Scam

on the

CAM

A Sesame Seade Mystery

CLÉMENTINE BEAUVAIS

Illustrated by
SARAH HORNE

Hodder
Children's
Books

A division of Hachette Children's Bo

FELLOWS' GARDEN

THIRD COURT

SECOND COURT

MASTER'S LODGE

MASTER'S GARDEN

FIRST COURT

PORTERS' LODGE

CHRIST'S COLLEGE

I

We had to win that race.

Not because there was anything exciting to win, like our own weight in candyfloss: teachers are just as stingy as parents. But because Julius Hawthorne and his crew from the Laurels School were in the other boat.

The problem was that they'd overtaken us approximately ten minutes before, shouting, 'Look at the cute little kids from Goodall! Don't damage the boat too much – it's ours, remember!'

It was. The Laurels, out of immense kindness (according to Mr Halitosis) or pity (according to us), were sharing their boats and oars with our school that term. Goodall School doesn't have

any boats; it barely has enough money to pay Mr Halitosis a decent salary, judging by his very economic use of toothpaste.

Anyway, a little bird was telling me that it would be difficult to catch up with the Laurels crew. That little bird was a tiny yellow duckling who was also racing us, and also beating us.

I stared glumly at my pathetically slow crew. Due to being perfectly useless at sports, but very good at bossing people around, I'd been made cox. Sitting at the back of the boat, facing the meanders of the dangerous river, I was responsible for the steering of the splendid ship and the survival of its seamen and seawomen, by shouting to them that they should row harder.

Gemma, sitting opposite me, was stroke, setting the rhythm for the rest of the crew. She was the only one who was actually motivated to win. Due to having recently developed a detestable crush on Julius Hawthorne, she was eager to impress the eye-scratchingly ugly boy. Behind her, Solal, Lily, Emerald, Ben, and,

at bow, Toby, were idly splashing along and staring at the landscape like a group of old-age pensioners on a Sunday outing.

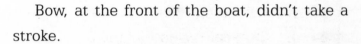

'Bow, take a stroke!' I commanded.

Bow, at the front of the boat, didn't take a stroke.

'Bow, take a stroke!' I shouted louder.

Bow still wasn't taking a stroke.

'Bow! Bow, do you copy? Take a stroke or else!'

(He said later that he'd been watching a very fast frog.)

'TOBY! Take a stroke, you useless sloth! We're heading straight to disas—'

I was unable to finish my sentence due to crashing into a weeping willow. This was only moderately fun, as everyone in the crew got ferociously whipped and strangled. Since I was

facing forwards, I swallowed a whole bunch of leaves in the manner of the bamboo-loving panda bear.

'So what does weeping willow taste like?' asked Gemma.

'Shut it!' I spluttered. 'All right, crew! Let's get started again or we'll lose the race. Everyone alive?'

'No,' said Emerald.

'Apart from Emerald, everyone alive?'

'Yes!' said everyone except for Toby.

'Bow, you alive? Bow? Toby? *Tobias Frederick Appleyard!* Your cox is talking to you!'

But Toby's voice emerged from the shady depths of the weeping willow jungle:

'Oh, give it a rest, Sesame! I've found a treasure!'

So, like a parliament of owls, everyone turned their necks one hundred and eighty degrees to look at Toby, who'd half-crashed into the bank. Underneath the cascade of willow leaves was the pirate chest.

'There are no pirate chests in Cambridge,' said Professor Seade (my mother).

'There are no pirate chests anywhere in the United Kingdom,' said Reverend Seade (my father).

'There are no pirate chests anywhere in Europe,' they both said.

'There *so* is. We *saw* it. It was just sitting there on the bank under the weeping willow near the University Boat House. And it was so heavy we couldn't move it – and it had an old, rusty lock – and it was chained up to the trunk of the willow, and it was so well-hidden that no one would ever have found it if Toby hadn't

been watching a frog instead of taking a stroke.'

'I have no idea what you're talking about,' said Mum, and Dad said, 'Me neither, as usual.'

'Why are you so anti-pirates? It would be the coolest thing if there were some in Cambridge!'

'Why are you nagging us with silly questions? Aren't you supposed to be playing with your friends? They're waiting for you in the garden.'

'I came in to see if there was anything we could munch on.'

Dad sighed and walked to the kitchen. He came back with a luscious-looking Bakewell tart, saying 'Don't eat it all!' (but accidentally we did).

When I hopped back out into the garden, Toby and Gemma were sitting underneath the big tree, which shed shattered sunlight all over them. They'd started drawing a map on my geography notebook, but Peter Mortimer had elected the notebook as his own particular throne and was spitting at them.

'Why does your cat hate us so much?' asked Gemma.

'He doesn't hate you, he's just shy,' I said, and just then Peter Mortimer reached out, scratched Gemma's arm, turned around, bit Toby's knee, and finally strutted away and climbed up the big tree.

'Right – what do we have here?' I asked.

'Toby thinks he saw an engraving on the chest,' said Gemma, 'just before Halitosis turned up to tell us off.'

We all shuddered. Mr Halitosis had been cycling along the bank on his creaky bike for just enough time for his entire T-shirt to be drenched in bile-yellow sweat. Five or six cows in the field behind him had galloped away at jaguar-speed when he'd arrived. Hardly had we laid hands on the pirate chest than he'd screamed at us from the other side of the river:

'You're a disgrace to Goodall School! What have you been doing? The Laurels crew passed the finish line twenty minutes ago!'

And that's why we'd had to abandon the treasure and row mournfully back to the Laurels' Boat House, where we'd found that

the winners had been carefully filling our shoes
with river weed.

'An engraving? Of what?' I asked.

'I don't know,' replied Toby, frowning in a
way that seemed painful. 'It looked like a crest.
Just above the lock.'

'Well, what was it? A mermaid? An octopus?
A skull and crossbones?'

'I can't remember.'

Gemma and I huffed and puffed so forcefully
that we ripped all the fluff off a bunch of white
dandelions. How's that for birthday cake
practice? Next time, I'll have twelve candles, so
I try to train whenever I can.

'Seriously, Toby, you're so disappointing,'
said Gemma. 'You were the closest to the
pirate chest. You *should* remember what that
engraving was.'

'Stop stressing me out! It's there in my head
somewhere,' pleaded Toby, 'but for some reason
the only things I can think about right now are
the lyrics to *Rule, Britannia* and the definition
of "peninsula".'

8

'OK – then we need to hypnotise you,' I said. 'Get up, everyone!'

We all jumped to our feet and I blindfolded Toby with my scarf before he could say 'wait a minute'.

'Sit down on this deck chair. We have to make you live that moment again – exactly as it was!'

'There's no river,' observed Gemma.

'Well observed,' I observed. 'However, we do have a small stream.'

The Master's Garden at Christ's College, Cambridge, which is where I live for parent-related reasons, has a stream at the bottom of it. I never approach it if I can avoid it, because it frizzes and slithers with disgusting fish, who I refuse to believe are vegetarian.

But when necessary, Sesame Seade, Cambridge's first self-made superheroine, puts away her fears. So we dragged the deck chair, with Toby in it, all the way to the fishy stream, and I can tell you he wasn't exactly light, and I can also tell you that Gemma wasn't putting

9

in all the effort she would have done if Julius Hawthorne had been there to watch.

We got there in the end, sweating and panting, and Toby said, 'Well, that was fun. Otherwise, we could have moved the deck chair, and I would have sat in it afterwards.'

I wondered why Gemma hadn't thought of that, and she looked at me like she was wondering why *I* hadn't.

'Right. Can you hear the water?' I asked.

'Yes, it's super relaxing. And what with that scarf covering my eyes, I think I might fall asleep.'

'You'd better not, you lazy dormouse,' I exclaimed, 'we haven't dragged you all the way here for you to get a little doze on the house. You need to remember what was engraved on the chest. Gemz – grab the deck chair and rock it slowly, to mimic the soft cradling of the rippling waves.'

'If she does that, there's absolutely no way I won't fall asleep,' declared Toby.

'I'll pinch him if he does,' said Gemma, and

Toby winced. I went to fetch a broomstick and stuck it in Toby's hands.

'What's that?'

'Your oar. Now everything is just like it was this morning.'

'Why are you whispering?'

'I'm trying to hypnotise you, Toby, remember?'

'Yeah, but whispers make me sleepy.'

'Pinch him, Gemma.'

'Ouch!'

'Now listen. You've crashed into a weeping willow, and half crashed into the bank. What's under the weeping willow?'

'A pirate chest.'

'Describe it to me.'

'It's made of wood with metallic bands and a metal lock. It's chained to the trunk of the tree.'

'Very good. What else?'

'You're shouting your head off in the cox box, and it's annoying me.'

'Yes, that's not important. What else?'

'I wonder where the frog is!'

'What frog?'

'The one I saw before we crashed.'

'Before *we* crashed?' exclaimed Gemma. '*We* didn't crash – *you* crashed *us*!'

'Shush, Gemma! You're going to ruin the deep hypnotic state! Never mind the frog, Toby.'

'It was a super strong frog, you know – it was swimming ultra fast!'

'I said, never mind the frog. What else can you see?'

'Ben's hair. It's really greasy. There's a louse

in it going up and down, up and down, like a little dolphin.'

'No, look at the bank, not at Ben. The pirate chest. What's on it?'

Dramatic silence. Gemma's still rocking the deck chair. The fish are still swimming in circles next to us, ready to pounce. Will Sesame Seade succeed as Cambridge's greatest hypnotist?

And suddenly everything happened at the same time:

'I know! I know! I remember!' screamed Toby.

'Sophie! Gemma! What on Earth are you doing to Toby?' screamed my parents.

'*Hakuna matata*!' screamed my ridiculous mobile phone, which is its way of telling me that someone is calling me.

So Toby leapt out of the deck chair and grabbed a pencil, my parents leapt out of the house and grabbed Gemma (she's not fast enough), and I leapt out of grabbing distance and grabbed my phone. It was, the screen said, Jeremy Hopkins – or rather, '*Susie*', as I call him in my phone's address book so as not to awaken

the suspicions of my parents. I climbed up the big tree and sat down next to Peter Mortimer.

'Hello?'

'Hi, Sesame, it's Jeremy.'

'I know,' I whispered. 'Listen, I can't talk to you for very long. I've found refuge on a branch, but Professor and Reverend Seade are prowling around the tree and looking up at me in the manner of a couple of growly grizzly bears who've located a beehive. Sticky situation.'

'Sounds terrifying. OK, I'll be quick: can I send you on a mission?'

'Of course! I haven't had one of those for ages. Well, three weeks. What do you need me to investigate?'

Through the leaves I could see Toby drawing and Gemma looking all nice to try and convince Mum and Dad that nothing strange had been happening at all. Apparently, she was succeeding, which didn't surprise me: she does wear pearl earrings.

'Well,' said Jeremy, 'there have been some

14

strange events in the lead-up to the Boat Race between Cambridge and Oxford. It's in less than two weeks now, and some rowers on the Cambridge team have been falling mysteriously ill.'

'Wicked! Arsenic? Cyanide?'

'I didn't say *dead*, I said ill. Ill enough that they can't take part in the race. Three of them so far have had to drop out. Bit of a strange coincidence, isn't it?'

I love coincidences. 'Indeed. What do you want me to do?'

'Well, the newspaper is going to run a story on that, of course, and we'd love to have some special revelations to make, as usual ...'

I could already picture the big red headlines of *UniGossip*: *Cambridge crew crushed by baffling bacteria!*

'Sounds good,' I said. 'So ... I go to the University Boat House and investigate?'

'Yes – we can't send a student there, they won't trust us. Why don't you go and pretend you're writing a cute little article for your cute

little school newspaper? They'll let you in and answer all your questions, and once you're in the place …'

'Say no more! I will sneak in and smuggle out all their dirty secrets, in the name of *UniGossip*!'

And I theatrically hung up, repocketed the phone, and slid down the big trunk all the way to the ground where Mum and Dad were beaming at Gemma as if she was God's gift to parents.

'What were you doing up that tree, Sophie?' asked Mum.

'Rummaging around for squirrel eggs.'

'Squirrels don't lay eggs: they are mammals,' said Dad.

'That explains why I couldn't find any. If they existed, though, do you think they'd be furry?'

'That's a ridiculous question,' Dad declared. And he and Mum both made their way to the house, which is what I'd been hoping for.

'Thought they'd never leave,' said Toby. 'Right, here's the drawing I've just done. Sesame, you're the awesomest hypnotist in the

world. Maybe you should do it as a job!'

'I can't,' I replied sadly, 'I'm already a superheroine. But I can keep it as a hobby.'

And we all looked at the drawing and went 'Wow!', because it was a true pirate engraving: a red crest with a round, golden, many-beamed rudder.

'Pirates,' I whispered, 'are among us.'

II

'Good afternoon, Sir. I'm very sorry to importune you in the midst of what I'm sure must be an extremely busy time for you, but allow me to introduce myself: my name is Gemma Sarland, Editor-in-Chief of the school newspaper *The Goodall Days*, and these are my friends and colleagues Toby and Sesame; and we would be immensely grateful if you would let us interview you and have a look around the Boat House for a special feature in next month's issue.'

Toby whistled. I have to admit I was quite impressed. 'Good job, Gemz! It's like you swallowed my mother for breakfast!'

'Should I flutter my eyelids a bit more?'

'No, your eyes are already barely more than a blur. But flash the pearl earrings. And don't forget to do that thing where you move your head and your hair stays exactly in place like you're a Lego figure.'

She frowned and crossed her arms, which proved that she wasn't a Lego figure.

'All right,' I said, 'your turn, Toby. You'll be the camera man.'

'Great! But I don't have a camera.'

'Not yet. But look what I borrowed from the real *Goodall Days* journalists.'

And I produced a huge camera with a telescopic zoom and as many buttons on it as there are warts on Mr Halitosis's chin.

'Wow,' Gemma marvelled. 'Amanda let you borrow the school paper's camera? After the damage you did last time you borrowed their printer?'

'How was I supposed to know it wouldn't print on lasagne sheets? They're just as thin as paper. Anyway, borrow is a big word. Let's say I'll put it back in the cupboard before she

notices it's gone. Catch, Toby!'

'Hey, don't give it to me! You know how clumsy I am! What if I break it?'

'I'm at least ten times as clumsy as you, so your having it will make its life expectancy longer by at least a few minutes. Anyway, the gist of it is – you go in and pretend to take lots of pictures while Gemma prattles on about the interview. Right. Let's go, team!'

'Wait a minute,' said Gemma, pointing at me. 'Who are you?'

'Who am I? Has your brain suddenly been abducted by an ill-advised brain-thief? I'm Sesame Seade, supersleuth on skates, Cambridge's first self-made superheroine! I'm almost internationally famous, feared by at least some criminals, and a couple of my adventures have even been written down by an amicable pen-pusher for clever people to read. There are as many connections in my brain as …'

'Shut it, Sesame. I mean – which part are you playing in this story? While I'm being important and journalistic, and while Toby's

merrily snapping away, what will you be doing?'

'Oh, *that*. I thought you'd guessed. You know how adults, sadly, never trust me?

'Yes,' chorused Toby and Gemma.

'Well, that's why I'll have to act extremely innocently. I'll keep looking at my shoes and shooting silly smiles at the walls. Just tell the rowers I'm the vaguely stupid kid in the class that you've been told to take along and acknowledge in the article so she can feel special for one day in her life.'

'Why can't I do that?' moaned Toby. 'I'm sure I'd be good at it.'

'No doubt. But don't worry, you'll be my inspiration. All right – let's get a move on!'

So we shot out of school on our faithful wheels: my purple roller-skates lashed with orange flames, Gemma's tidy little scooter and Toby's red bike. The problem when we race through town like that is that we're a little bit faster than the speed of sound and it's happened a few times that we've run over various people, some of them notorious criminals. Just like

today, when there was a CLANG! and a BANG! and two OUCHES! and when the dust cloud finally settled it revealed a very red Gemma and a very black-and-blue ...

'Julius Hawthorne!' I exclaimed. 'What are *you* doing here?'

'What do you mean?' he scoffed, dusting his embroidered school blazer. 'This is my city too, you know. I was peacefully making my way home from the Laurels.'

Gemma beamed at him like he'd just said he was walking back from Hogwarts.

'I'm ever so sorry,' she said. 'I hope you don't have too many bruises.'

'Bruises?' he replied.

22

'Oh, you mean haematomas. Yes, a few, but I should be fine. We Laurel boys are made of ferromolybdenum.'

'Can you move out of the way of Gemma's wheels?' I asked. 'We're trying to get somewhere to do something.'

'Oh yes? Riverwards? What might it be?'

He scrunched up his eyes in a perfect imitation of Peter Mortimer having swallowed anti-worm medicine. 'Perhaps training in secret, in the hope that you might one day beat us at rowing? Surely not?'

'Actually,' I said sourly, 'not quite. We're going there to interview the Cambridge University Rowing Team for the school newspaper.'

'Are you now? Did you arrange that with Gwendoline, the coach?'

'Course. We're best mates. She and us are like that.'

And I showed my hand with four fingers all intertwined, which is quite difficult, if you want to take a moment to try it yourself.

'Funny,' snarled Julius. 'She hasn't told me

anything about you. Even though I see her every evening, since she's, you know, my *sister*.'

I have to admit I got a little bit warm around the ears, judging by my hair getting all lifted up by the steam in the manner of a hot air balloon. Before I could think of a good lie, Julius waved and said, 'Anyway, catch up later. Probably at the next race. I'm sorry I never see any of you for terribly long; it's all a bit of a blur. I do try to slow up my crew, but it's very unnatural for them to go so painfully sluggishly.'

And he was gone. I sped up to avoid having to listen to Gemma's reproaches about my ruining her chances of ever being recognised by Julius Hawthorne as anything other than a loser.

'Your parents ruined them first by putting you at Goodall,' replied Toby shrewdly.

We reached the big field at the north of the town and whooshed past a cluster of cows, spiralled around a few dogs tied to pushchairs tied to people, sped up at the white-and-pink bridge beside which the weeping willow was

still weeping, and a few seconds later braked in front of the University Boat House. Just in time to avoid diving into the grey-green Cam.

Next to us was a huge, shiny white rowing boat, and on the bank were long black oars decorated with the light blue stripes of Cambridge. Examining the oars was a skinny, small brown-haired student with glasses who looked nothing like a rower. He looked up when he heard us, and I switched to stupid mode (which is a very difficult mode for me to switch to).

'Can I help you?' he asked kindly. 'Are you lost?'

Gemma's hand shot out towards his. 'Good afternoon, Sir. I'm very sorry to importune you ...'

And we were in.

It turned out that the student's name was Will Sutcliffe, and that he was a student at Homerton College and the cox of the University Rowing Team. He was about as tall as me and barely heavier, and he had a smile as white as

the boat, and almost as big, which punctured his cheeks with two dimples.

'A school article on the University Team! Sure, we'll find some time to answer your questions, of course,' he went on, taking us on a whistle-stop tour of the Boat House. 'We've just finished a short outing on the river, we were just practising starts. We're going to have a debriefing session right now, with Gwen – the coach – she's probably going to come down in a minute ...'

As he was opening and shutting doors and showing us around the smelly gym, the smelly changing-rooms and the smelly offices, Gemma

was busy taking notes and asking questions that Will didn't really need to fuel his endless chitchat. Toby, meanwhile, was taking so many pictures that I worried for a moment that the camera would melt. As for me, I was acting perfectly stupid, but my constellation of brain cells was taking in as much as possible.

And in particular the grotesque amount of bottles of antibacterial gel screwed to the walls, with handwritten inscriptions on Post-It notes above them – 'Keep your hands clean!' 'Bacteria spread in every handshake!' and other such instructions which my parents would have

been proud to give.

While Will was taking us up a smelly staircase, I nudged Gemma and pointed at one of them. She nodded.

'Will?' she asked innocently. 'What's all that about? Have you all been getting a cold, or measles, or the bubonic plague?'

'Oh, no,' he said, suddenly sombre. 'There's been an outbreak of norovirus, or something of the sort. Three of our best rowers have come down with a terrible stomach illness and can't make the race. It's all a bit hush-hush, but it won't hurt if it ends up in your school newspaper – as long as you publish the article after the race.'

'What's norovirus?' asked Gemma.

'Some stomach bug, probably from the river. But it's not the usual type, apparently. We're not sure. The guys who've caught it got extremely ill for about a week. When they're up and running again, it's too late, of course – they've lost too much weight and been out of practice for too long. They've had to give up, and we've pulled guys from the reserve crew. Pretty bad news for the team. Anyway, we're doing our best. They have to wash their hands all the time. Everyone's got their own personal tube of antibacterial gel!'

He got his out of his pocket and shook it under our noses.

'What's going on, Wally? Who are those kids? Your schoolfriends?'

We'd reached the top of the staircase, but we still had to crane our necks to look at the boy who'd just spoken. And even looking up like that we couldn't quite make out the features of a face which was so high up in the distance that it was probably less oxygenated than the rest of us.

'Oh, hi, Rob,' Will laughed. 'You're funny – no, they're just kids from a local school who want to run a story on the University Team in their newspaper. I told them they could ask a few questions.'

'Sure,' scoffed the giant, 'best idea I've ever heard. Like we've got time to waste, when

we're trying to get everything together before next week.'

And he walked away with T-Rex-like footsteps, making the whole Boat House shake.

Will smiled awkwardly.

'Rob Dawes,' he said to us, 'is in the reserve crew. He's, um, quite a character.'

'Why does he call you Wally?' asked Toby.

'Oh,' said Will, 'just because, well, I guess ...'

'Because he looks exactly like Wally in *Where's Wally?*,' said a voice just behind us. 'Do you also want to say that in your school newspaper?'

We twirled around and were faced with what Julius Hawthorne would have looked like in eight years' time with a short, curly blonde wig. We guessed that this probably meant we were now facing Gwendoline Hawthorne.

'Ah, Gwen,' said Will. 'Yes,' he chuckled to us, 'it's Martin, one of our rowers, well, one of our ex-rowers – he got the virus – who found that nickname for me. Funny, huh? And, you know, everyone now calls me—'

'Can we have that debriefing session?' snapped Gwendoline. 'Or do you have an interview planned with the local kindergarten?'

'Sure,' said Will, 'sure – are the guys ready?'

'They're waiting for you. We're all waiting.'

'Okey-doke, sorry – coming, coming,' said Will in his singsong voice. 'Sorry, kids – meeting time. Everyone's a bit stressed because of the dropouts, you see. We can't have anyone else there, meetings are top-secret. What if you're spies sent from Oxford, you know? Haha! Just kidding. Maybe I'll see you around some other time? Sorry again. Feel free to drop by if you have any more questions. Bye-bye! Bye-bye!'

He showed us out and vanished again into the staircase. The white boat was gently tapping along the bank, next to a couple of angry-looking swans. Propelled by our splendid muscles and by hunger, we got back to mine and settled down on my bed with mugs of hot chocolate and hot-cross buns.

'Well,' said Gemma, 'we haven't learnt much,

apart from the fact that everyone's stressed out about the virus.'

'I've taken some way cool pictures with that telescopic zoom, though,' said Toby. 'Look – that's Gemma's earwax!'

We looked, and it wasn't pretty. Toby swooshed through a dozen random pictures.

'What's that one?' I asked. 'Looks like it was taken through a half-open door.'

'Dunno. Oh, yeah, it's Gwendoline's office, I think.'

'Can you zoom in?'

He pressed the screen.

And then Gemma said, 'What's that old metal key on the desk?'

And then Toby said, 'Why is there an Oxford University bag in there?'

III

I'll say something for Mr Halitosis: when he's got an idea, he sticks to it. He sticks to it almost as much as his sweaty shirts stick to his chest (but not quite as much as his bogeys stick to the end of his nose). The next morning, just as we were walking into the classroom all porridged-up and yawning, he welcomed us with a formidable roar.

'This afternoon after class, children, you're going to the river with me and rowing and rowing until you get good enough to beat the Laurels boys!'

'That's not super convenient, Mr Barnes,' I said, 'because Gemma, Toby and I had plans for this afternoon.'

'Such as what, Sophie Seade?' he asked, getting dangerously close to my airspace. 'What kind of havoc were you going to wreak this time?'

'None whatsoever,' I said. 'We're writing an article for the *Goodall Days*. On the University Rowing Team.'

'You three doing something productive? I don't believe a word of it. And that wouldn't dispense you from training. You'll be in pairs: Gemma and Sophie, Toby and Lily, Emerald and Solal.'

'In *pairs*?' I choked. 'You're expecting me to *row*?'

'A little bit of exercise won't do you any harm, my dear child,' said Mr Halitosis. '*Mens sana in corpore sano*: a healthy mind in a healthy body. That's what one should always strive for.'

'And failing that, become a primary school teacher,' I muttered. 'All right, team – we need to talk.'

Except we couldn't, because class had started, and we had to resort to the good old

34

strategy of passing little notes around, which was all the more complicated as it was Dictation time.

'A smorgasbord of heterogeneous epithets,' dictated Mr Halitosis, 'was the ubiquitous idiosyncrasy of this metaphysician's phraseology ...'

OK, I pencilled on the lines of my music notebook. *This afternoon, Toby, you keep Halitosis occupied. Gemz and I will go and investigate the Boat House and elucidate that Oxford bag question.*

'... but his pseudo-gnostic logorrhoea, full

of mammoth anacolutha and pachydermic pleonasms ...'

No need, wrote Gemma hurriedly in bright red ink on the music sheet. *I've figured out why Gwen's got an Oxford bag.*

Why?? added Toby in fountain pen.

'... was, per se, siphoned of all signified, and, qua *paideia*, superfetatory and sans *sprezzatura* ...'

Yesterday, replied Gemma, getting as red as her ink, *I looked her up on the Internet. She went to university in Oxford. She's coaching the Cambridge team now, but there's nothing surprising with her still owning an Oxford bag.*

What????!!! wrote Toby, who's got a soft spot for exclamation and question marks. *She's an ex-Oxford student????? Well, if that's not a motive to want the whole Cambridge team to fail!!!!!*

And he added a whole line of !s to the music sheet, which made it look like an uninspired composer had gone brutally insane.

'... which both bamboozled and flummoxed,

36

but also galvanised, the zealous areopagus of his exegetes.'

That's a ridiculous claim, wrote Gemma, redder now than the ink. *She's the team's coach, she'd have no reason to want them to lose.*

'All done?' thundered Mr Halitosis. 'Three seconds to check that you've written your name on your sheet, and I'm collecting them!'

Toby panicked, quickly scribbled 'Tobais Aplepleyard' at the top of his sheet, and completed the dictation with whatever he could remember, ending up with 'both bamboos and hammocks are jealous of Exeter'.

'Well,' I whispered to Gemma and Toby as Mr Halitosis was touring the classroom wrenching dictation sheets from everyone, 'whether that's true or not, I'd still like to have a look at that office. And to see if that old metal key might fit into, you know ...'

'... the pirate chest,' completed Toby.

☆☆☆

37

'Sesame, you are relentlessly hopeless.'

'I'm trying my best!'

'Try harder! You're going to crash us into a barge. Take a small stroke. A SMALL stroke!'

Plonk.

'Well, at least now we're next to the bank.'

'Only the tip of the boat is touching it. Take another stroke!'

'No, wait – if I reach out to the bank, I can pull us in …'

'Careful! You're going to tip us oveeeer—'

A couple of minutes and a century later, under the sarcastic gaze of our two swan acolytes, we managed to moor our small rowing-boat to the bank. We made sure that it was hidden from the other side of the river by the hippie hair of the weeping willow, and got off.

The pirate chest was still there, and still locked.

'I hope Toby's doing his best to keep Halitosis angry at the other end of the river,' murmured Gemma as we tiptoed behind the silent Boat Houses.

'Don't worry. He's a natural. Duck!'

'Sesame, we can't waste time looking at the ducks.'

'No, I mean – duck! There are people coming!'

I grabbed her by the collar and we dived down into a bush. The University Team, including the ever-smiley Will, the grim-looking Rob, and Gwendoline the snow queen, were all getting into a van. I guessed they were going to Ely to train on the river there.

'Excellent,' I said as the van roared past us and disappeared into the distance, 'there won't be anyone in there. Let's go!'

All the doors on the Boat House were locked, which was a happy occurrence as I'd been yearning for an opportunity to climb up buildings. We made our way to the back of the house, found a drainpipe, then a diagonal wooden beam, and a few minutes later we were on the little balcony at the front of the house. Someone had left a small window open, probably hoping to empty the house of some of its smelliness, and we squeezed inside disappointingly easily.

'I hope they close it next time,' I said, 'it will give me an excuse to use my skeleton key.'

The house was dark and silent. We'd landed in the changing-rooms, full of discarded towels, water-bottles, and men's underwear which we didn't look at. There were also boxes of biscuits and chocolates, which I managed not to steal from (because Gemma held my hands behind my back), and a smorgasbord of heterogeneous items including more bottles of antibacterial gel, a red-and-white stripy hat, a Cambridge teddy bear, and a discarded copy of *UniGossip*.

'This way,' I whispered to Gemma, and we walked into Gwendoline's office. The old metal key wasn't on the desk any more, but we soon found it hanging from a little hook next to the door.

It fell into my pocket.

As for the Oxford bag, it was still on a chair, but didn't contain anything at all. 'Anything else of interest?' I asked Gemma, who was looking around.

'No. I'm telling you, you're completely

wrong. There's no reason why Gwendoline should be up to no good. She's the coach, she wants them to win!'

'Well, let's see if that key fits into that chest, and then we'll decide. You're right, maybe it's completely innocent. Maybe she just keeps her clothes there. Or a body chopped into several pieces.'

I dodged Gemma's incendiary glare (it ricocheted off the wall, left through the window and set a branch of a nearby tree on fire), and we wormed our way out of the house through the changing-room window again. A few acrobatic moves later, we were about to touch the ground, ready to run to the weeping willow and what might be a perfectly innocent pirate chest.

Except we couldn't run, because we couldn't touch the ground.

Because we were hovering in midair.

Caught by the very sturdy, very hairy, and very angry arms of someone whose deep and thunderous voice in our ears said, with a strong accent:

'Eh bien! Finally, I've found you, you damned zieves!'

Painfully, I managed to turn my head around to look at our captor.

And I must confess I trembled a little.

Because he had a gold earring, and a beard, and long hair, and a red bandana. I've been in tricky situations before, as you may or may not remember.

But never before had I been kidnapped by an authentic pirate.

IV

Legs still dangling in the air, we were taken by the pirate to his ship. But rather than a fearsome caravel, it was a barge on the side of the river.

And rather than a skull and crossbones, it was flying a French flag and a Union Jack.

And rather than being called *Slaughterer of the Seven Seas*, it was called *La Sardine Souriante*, which, vague memories of French lessons with Mademoiselle Corentin told me, meant *The Smiling Sardine*.

There wasn't a shadow of a sardine anywhere on the barge, however. But there was a rotund pirate woman fixing something on the roof, and a small pirate child who was playing with a chocolate-brown labrador on the plank.

'I've found the zieves!' declared the pirate to his wife.

'What do you mean?' she laughed, looking at us. 'Marcel, those are children!'

'I caught zem hand in ze bag!'

'Not true,' I said, 'you caught us as we were making our way down from the balcony.'

'It's a French expression,' the pirate lady explained. 'He means red-handed. Marcel, seriously, what's that about? Put them down.'

'Zey'd broken into ze University Boat House,' he said, and he put us down on the ground.

'But look,' said his wife, 'they can't be the thieves. They're way too young. And the one we spotted last time was definitely a boy.'

'Zey could have accomplices,' said Marcel.

'We're completely not thieves,' I said.

'See, we don't even have a bag or anything with us.'

'Empty your pockets!' said the pirate.

Gemma and I grimaced. In my pocket was the key. What if he guessed I'd stolen the key? What if it was the key to his pirate chest? What if Gwendoline had stolen the key from him to start with? I had to think even faster than Peter Pan.

'Tell me – did the thief look like that?' I asked, randomly pointing into the distance.

Everyone turned around to look, and I flung the key into the Cam. It disappeared with a little plop.

'Not at all,' said the pirate, 'zat would be completely absurd.'

And indeed it would, as the passer-by I'd accidentally designated was an old lady in an electric wheelchair with a tartan blanket on her lap.

'Ah well,' I said, 'I was just trying to help. But no, look, I've got nothing in my pockets.'

Gemma turned hers inside-out too, and

45

the pirate lady said to her husband, 'You see, darling, it can't be them.'

'What's that about, anyway?' I asked. 'Have there been thefts around the area recently?'

'Oh, yes,' said the pirate lady. 'Lots of burglaries in the barges. Some of my old jewellery was stolen, and Marcel's watch, and even some electronic equipment. And it's happened to many other people in barges along this corner of the river.'

'Have you told the police?' said Gemma.

'Of course,' smiled the woman. 'But they're not too concerned with what happens to people like us, it seems.'

'Do you know anything about pirate chests?' I asked.

'Pirate chests?' repeated Marcel, and he burst out laughing. 'We might look like pirates, but we're not, *ma petite fille.*'

That was extremely disappointing, but also meant we weren't in immediate danger of being made to walk the plank.

'OK,' I said, 'it was really nice to meet you.

Thanks for everything. I hope you catch your zieves. And now we need to run, or else our teacher will skin us alive with a nail file.'

'Wow,' said Gemma as we walked back to our rowing-boat. 'That was close. Where did you put the key?'

'I had to throw it into the river.'

'What? Are you mad?'

'Well, what else was I supposed to do with it? Swallow it? I wouldn't have looked forward to getting it back at the other end.'

'But now we don't have it any more!'

'Well observed. But it can't be helped, I'm afraid.'

Glumly, Gemma started fiddling with her ears, which is what she does when she's being all pensive and intellectual. Suddenly, in the manner of an opera diva, she screamed, 'Heavens! My earrings!'

'What about them?'

'My pearl earrings!'

'Yes, I know what they're made of. Everyone in the world knows.'

'They're gone!'

I looked at her ears, and indeed there were no pearls bulging from them to indicate that she was a respectable young girl.

'Are you sure you were wearing them today?' I asked. 'Thinking about it, I don't remember seeing them this morning.'

'I always wear them,' she said. 'I never take them off.'

'Seriously, Gemz, this morning I thought – there's something different about Gemma Sarland today. She's the same, and yet different. She's herself, and yet strangely Other. It was the earrings, I'm sure. You must have left them at home.'

She shook her head, but looked unsure.

'I'll check tonight,' she said, 'but I doubt it. I think I lost them at the Boat House.'

'Maybe they fell off when the pirate captured us.'

'He wasn't a pirate, he was a French barge-owner. He's a person just like us, and his life choice is just as good as all other life choices.

You've got to stop calling him a pirate, it's highly insulting.'

Having thus proven that losing her pearl earrings hadn't deprived her of random bouts of weirdness, she got back into the boat and we haphazardly rowed back to the Laurels' Boat House.

Toby was standing outside pretending to look innocent, which we immediately guessed meant he had hidden a frog inside his hoodie pocket.

'Have you hidden a frog inside your hoodie pocket, Toby?' I asked as we brushed past him carrying the boat on our shoulders.

'Yes,' he said. 'So, how did your mission go? I kept Halitosis very busy, just like you asked. I almost capsized us three times, and one of those on purpose. Lily was furious. As for Halitosis, he's currently trying to calm himself down.'

He pointed at Halitosis, who was lying under a nearby tree and breathing into a paper bag.

We all spared a minute to pray that the paper from the bag wouldn't ever end up recycled into any kind of food wrapping.

'The mission went quite badly,' I said. 'We stole the key, but got kidnapped by a pirate who was a French barge-owner and called us zieves, so we had to throw the key into the Cam, and as a result we couldn't open the chest which didn't belong to the pirate anyway, since he wasn't one.'

'Tough luck,' said Toby sympathetically.

'And I lost my earrings,' said Gemma.

'Oh yes,' said Toby, 'I was going to ask you where they were when you arrived this morning, and then I forgot.'

'This morning?' repeated Gemma. 'I didn't have them on when I got to school?'

'I told you!' I told her. 'You'll find them at home tonight, and since absence makes the heart grow fonder you'll love them even more than before. And who knows, they might have made lots of tiny baby pearls when you weren't watching.'

But Gemma wasn't listening: she was looking into the distance with an expression of such pain that I suspected for a minute the imminent arrival of the Four Horsemen of Apocalypse. But when I turned around I realised it was much less exciting than that; it was, in fact, the pangs of despised love. For yonder near the stream were Julius Hawthorne and Lily Murray (Toby's unfortunate rowing partner and owner of an impressive marmalade mesh of red hair) who were laughing and cooing together, gazing at each other from the corner of their long-lashed eyes in the manner of two badly drawn Disney princesses.

'I can't believe this,' said Gemma. 'She can't even play Dvořák on the cello.' I left her to her lovelorntate, because I was quite keen to have a look at Toby's frog. It was a lovely shade of green, like my mum's face when she gets the bill for something I've broken, and had two perfectly humid eyes, just like Mum again when she's signing the cheque to pay the bill.

'It's super fast, you know,' said Toby, stroking

its sleek back. 'I'm sure it's faster than any frog I've ever seen.'

'I didn't know you were in the habit of speed-checking amphibians,' I said. 'Where did you catch it?'

'Oh, next to the University Boat House, when we finally passed by it earlier. You must have been inside then.'

While we were playing with the frog, Mr Halitosis awoke from his paper bag-induced calm, got to his feet, and threatened to slice us into slim strips of meat for a giant stir-fry if we weren't ready to go back to Goodall in two seconds. Not being one for soy sauce, I rushed into the Laurels' Boat House to get my clothes and bag.

As I checked my phone, coming out into the sunshine, I saw that I had a lovely little text waiting from me from *Susie*, all warm and exciting like a mini-blueberry muffin: *Fourth & fifth rowers of the University Team taken ill and in hospital. How's the investigation going? Jeremy x*

Running back to Toby and Gemma, I found the latter sidekick in a state of dangerous hyperventilation, repeating, 'He came to talk to me! He came to talk to me!'

'Who did?' I asked.

'Julius!'

'Caesar?'

'No, Hawthorne!'

'Ah,' I said. 'Maybe he guessed you could play Dvořák in the end.'

'He told me he'd only come here to talk to me! He knew that we were training, and he wanted to talk to me! He came here to talk to me!'

'To say what?' asked Toby.

'Just that,' said Gemma.

'He came here just to tell you that he'd come here just to talk to you?'

'Yes!' she marvelled. 'Isn't that wonderful?'

'The boy is profoundly deranged, as I always suspected,' I said. 'But that's OK, since he seems to have found an equally insane kindred spirit.'

'And then,' reminisced Gemma, 'I asked

him if he could give me his phone number, and he did!'

Toby and I tried to be as discreet as possible while we hiccoughed and retched and went, 'Urgh! argh! disgusting! yuck!', but I think Gemma still heard us.

In short, that day was a huge failure.

'In short, today is a huge failure,' I informed Peter Mortimer in the living-room. 'We lost a key that wasn't ours, didn't learn anything new about the virus, some more rowers fell ill, and Gemma's lost all her brainpower due to *l'amour.*'

Peter Mortimer seemed quite sympathetic:

he tried to pat my shoulder, but forgot to retract his claws. When I'd finished blotting the blood with the ivory tablecloth, Dad and Mum walked into the living-room carrying plates and cutlery for my dinner (and theirs).

'I'm completely and utterly fed up with Sophie,' said Mum. 'I just wish our paths would never cross again. I certainly don't want to help her any more; I've given her all the time and effort I can.'

'You're absolutely right, my dear,' said Dad. 'She's tried your patience enough. It's not your responsibility. Just tell her to go away.'

I thought that was a bit cheeky of them.

'It *is* your responsibility!' I claimed. 'At least until I'm eighteen. We still have to endure one another for another six and a half years, I'm afraid. And I won't go away – at least not until I've had my dinner, and only if Peter Mortimer can come with me.'

'We're not talking about *you*, Sophie,' sighed Mum. 'We're talking about another Sophie.'

'Oh, I see. I did think it was a bit silly of you to go trumpeting it around the house that you were going to get rid of me. If I conspired with my husband to abandon my daughter, I'd talk about it very quietly and probably in a secret code of my invention.'

'The problem with Sophie is that she's a paranoid little Mithridate,' sighed Dad.

'Which Sophie are we talking about now?' I inquired.

'You,' said Dad.

'Calling me Sesame would make it immediately clearer. What's the deal with the other Sophie?'

They sat down in silence and started to eat

56

their chicory and walnut salad like they do when they don't want to reply to my questions. So I resorted to singing my question to the tune of *Jingle Bells*, which ended up sounding like this:

What's the deal, what's the deal,
with the other Soph?
What's the deal, oh what's the deal,
with the o-o-other Soph?
OH! What's the deal, what's the deal,
with the other Soph?
What's the deal, oh what's the deal,
with the O-O-Other Soph?

This was a good day, as I only had to sing it four and a half times, increasing the volume every time, until Mum gave in.

'Hush! You're giving everyone a migraine! The "deal", as you distastefully put it, is something absolutely uninteresting to you. Sophie Quentin is a doctor at Addenbrookes Hospital. She wants me to look at a certain virus that is affecting some people. They don't know what it is and want my pharmacological expertise. But I don't have the time to look at it closely. Satisfied?'

'Who's ill?' I asked.

They didn't reply, so I started to sing again – 'Who is ill, who is ill' – but immediately Mum said, 'I'm not allowed to tell you, it's a secret. Eat your chicory.'

'I hate chicory. Anyway, it's OK, *maman adorée*, I know it's the rowers. It's not norovirus then?' I asked.

Mum's eyes widened so much I worried her eyelids might swallow up her glasses. 'I don't know how you know that,' she said, 'but no, it's

not norovirus. Finish your chicory.'

'I hate chicory.'

'Finish it.'

'If I finish my chicory, can I ask what you think it is?'

She nodded, so I wolfed down the rest of the chicory in five seconds (I actually adore chicory with an ardent passion; I just pretend I don't so I can have a conveniently pleasant way of pressuring parents. It is a strategy I warmly recommend.)

'That was revolting,' I said. 'Never give me chicory again. So, what do you think it is?'

'I think,' said Mum pensively, 'that it's a man-made virus. And I don't think it's in the river. I think ... I think someone is poisoning those poor rowers. Yes, poisoning them.'

V

'I don't know,' said Gemma, 'how it's possible that I'm both immensely happy and completely unhappy.'

'It happens to me when I eat After Eights,' said Toby, 'because I'm like, "wow! chocolate!" and then "yuck! mint!", and it's really confusing.'

'Right. That's not quite what I'm talking about,' said Gemma. 'I'm devastated, because I can't find my earrings. They weren't anywhere at home yesterday, I looked everywhere. I must have lost them some time the day before yesterday. They must have fallen off. Maybe here, at school.'

'Maybe they've fallen inside your ears!' suggested Toby. 'They might be trapped in all

the earwax that we saw you had.'

'Earwax!' exclaimed Gemma. 'Toby, do you still have those pictures from the other day?'

'Sure,' he said, 'I downloaded them all on to my phone.'

He got his phone out and swished through a hundred pictures of his frog that he'd taken the evening before, until he got to the shots from the University Boat House. 'Here's the earwax one,' he said.

'Unmistakably earringed,' I said. 'You must have lost them some time after then.' Toby slid his finger on the screen. On the next picture – Gemma talking to Will – she was still wearing them. The next few pictures were a bit of staircase, Rob's foot, and Gwen's office. And then Gemma again, talking to me. He zoomed in.

'No earrings!' he said. 'You lost them on the staircase.'

'It must have been when I was looking up at Rob,' she murmured. 'OK, well, at least I know where they are. I'll go this evening after

school and try to see if I can find them. Want to come along?'

Toby nodded, but I replied sadly, 'Unfortunately my parents are forcing me to come along with them to some extravaganza at St Catharine's College. They don't want to leave me home alone as they don't trust me to keep it an animal-free zone. Let me know how it goes, though!'

'St Catharine's!' exclaimed Gemma. 'That reminds me why I'm unbelievably happy. I saw Julius this morning! We met up on the way to school.'

We let her stare into the sky for a few minutes, until the bell rang and we had to walk upstairs to our classroom.

'What's the link between Julius and St Catharine's, anyway?' I asked, shaking her out of her reverie.

'Oh, yes,' she said. 'He told me that Gwendoline is a student at St Catharine's, so he goes there to visit her all the time. Oh, and Rob Dawes is also a student there. Do

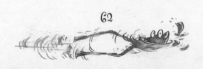

you know, apparently everyone *hates* Rob Dawes. And Julius doesn't trust him either. The other day, Julius saw Rob mixing weird stuff into the rowers' food when he thought no one was looking. Being in the reserve crew, it would make sense for Rob to poison people to get into the first crew, so Julius thinks Rob is poisoning the rowers. Anyway, that's the link.'

'Wait – WHAT?' I shouted, and then realised everyone else had gone silent, waiting for Mr Halitosis to start telling us about the Tudors.

'Sophie Seade!' he groaned. '*Primo*, one doesn't say "what?" when one is polite; one says "I beg your pardon?". *Secundo*, I've had enough of your mumbling, bumbling, rumbling little clique. Tobias, go sit next to Victoria. Gemma, stay where you are. Sophie, you're coming to the front row – right in front of me, so I can keep an eye on you. Not a word!'

Everyone crossed themselves and looked down respectfully as I gloomily made my way to the front of the classroom, where chances

of survival are low due to the rarity of breathable air.

I sat down wondering if it was possible for a human being with no known mermaid ancestry to hold her breath for fifty-five minutes. I tried anyway. After all, as Mum told me (when Dad wasn't around to contest her version with a Bible in hand), everyone is descended from fish-like things. Maybe if the situation was perilous enough I could summon some gills from the dawn of time.

'Ah, Sophie, by the way,' said Mr Halitosis, turning around from the smartboard.

'Hmm?' I said, letting some of my precious air escape my nostrils.

'"Hmm" is not an appropriate way of acknowledging that someone is talking to you,'

he grumbled. 'Anyway – after you told me that you, Toby and Gemma were writing an article on the University Team for *The Goodall Days*, I got in touch with their cox and was extremely surprised to hear that this was not, in fact, another one of your lies.'

I nodded vigorously. I really couldn't afford to waste any more air.

'I'm very pleased about this,' said Mr Halitosis. 'I look forward to reading your article. And to make it even better, I've arranged with their cox for you three to accompany them to Ely on their daily outing tomorrow afternoon.'

I managed a big smile and a double thumbs-up.

'That is definitely not an acceptable response either!' whinged Mr Halitosis. 'You are incomprehensible. One minute you're screaming your head off, the next you've gone as dumb as the Little Mermaid. Anyway, back to the Tudors.'

And as he turned back to the smartboard, I discreetly dived down under the desk to

breathe in some less contaminated air.

There was cauliflower gratin for lunch. It looked like human brains in a sauce made from pug dribble, and tasted just a little bit less nice. Toby, whose dad had cooked the dreadful concoction, was blissfully finishing Gemma's plate after licking mine clean. 'I can't believe it,' I said. 'Why on Earth would Julius tell you that he thinks Rob is poisoning everyone?'

'He and I have no secrets from each other,' said Gemma dreamily.

'But it makes no sense! Will said it was a virus in the river. There's no reason why anyone in the crew should think it's purposeful poisoning.'

'Well, he's guessed. He's clever like that.'

'Why tell *you*, though?'

'I understand why you're jealous, Sess,' said Gemma. 'But one day you too will find someone like him to tell you secrets, I promise.'

66

I shook with horror at the thought of a Julius Hawthorne replica muttering things into my ear. 'No, but I mean, why should he tell you and not his sister, or the police?'

'Maybe he has. I'm sure he's done everything he thinks is right.'

'Indubitably,' I sniggered. 'It's very weird. Anyway, since I'm going to St Cat's tonight, I'll try to leave the parents somewhere and sneak into Rob Dawes's room. What are you doing, Toby?'

'Just saving a little bit for my frogs,' he replied, conscientiously scraping some brains into his pencil-sharpener. 'I've got another one now, I caught it in the pond behind the school. They're getting on great together.'

One sidekick lost to love, the other to frog-rearing. As usual, I was alone with my mission.

If your parents are anything like mine, they probably think you should permanently look three years younger than you are, but act forty years older. This is why I was made, that evening,

to wear a red corduroy dress, a ridiculous metal hairclip with a flower on it, and tiny shoes, but asked to revise my French grammar, geographical vocabulary, and advanced maths in order to be able to converse with the erudite people of St Catharine's as if I was just as old and wrinkled as them.

'And sit up, for goodness' sake, remember to sit up,' said Mum for the hundredth time as we walked into St Cat's.

'I will. You look uniquely gorgeous tonight, mesmerising mother,' I said. 'That coral necklace is super tip-top.'

'Thanks,' Mum muttered.

'Of course, it's extremely bad to wear coral. Did you know coral is an animal? *Viz*, you're currently wearing a dead animal. Plus, it's an endangered one. Most of the coral in the world is already dying, and with it all the sealife thingies that live in it. So because of your necklace, lots of little fishes are dead right now, or going "I don't feel very well today, due to lack of coral".'

'Yes, thank you, Sophie,' said Mum.

'Don't worry, though. All that aquatic slaughter is justified. You're the hottest momma on the block with that necklace.'

'David,' said Mum to Dad, 'please tell your daughter to be quiet.'

'Be quiet, Sophie,' said Dad, and we walked into Formal Hall.

Formal Halls, in case you don't know, are huge dining halls in Colleges, where profs and students eat when they feel like having long, tedious conversations with one another, all wearing black gowns. This is instead of staying home dipping fish fingers in  ketchup while reading detective stories, which is what I'll do every evening of my life from the minute I turn eighteen.

As I was sitting down, my phone vibrated in my pocket. I looked at it discreetly: it was a text from Gemma, saying,

Toby & I went to University Boat House tonight. No trace of earrings. Also, pirate chest mysteriously disappeared xx

I was just composing a response when an old lady exclaimed, sitting down next to me, 'Ah! You must be Agnes and David's daughter, Sophie!'

'Not Sophie,' I replied, 'Sesame.'

'Oh, I beg your pardon,' she said, shaking my hand. 'It must be your sister they told me about – a clever but devilishly uncontrollable little girl, from what I understand.'

'Oh yes,' I sighed, 'she's a handful, bless her. We have to keep her constantly locked up. But she's got cryptic crosswords to keep her busy, and we give her slices of meat to munch on through the bars of her cage three times a day.'

'Gracious heavens!' the lady cried.

That's when I noticed something familiar about the plates and the cutlery.

That familiar thing was the college crest, engraved on to them.

And that college crest was unmistakably the round, gold, many-beamed rudder that Toby had drawn from his hypnotic memories of the pirate chest.

'And what are you doing in class these days, my dear child?' inquired the lady next to me.

Still trying to figure out why the pirate chest would have the crest of St Cat's on it, I explained I was at an edgy school with a very modern curriculum comprising Carpentry, Ancient Aztec and Geography of Saturn. While she marvelled, I was keeping an eye on my parents, whose glasses of wine kept getting refilled by a watchful waiter. When the port arrived, they were both as rosy as Mum's coral necklace of death, and Dad had started talking in spoonerisms.

It was time to slip out.

'If you'll excuse me,' I murmured to my neighbour, 'I should very much like to pay a visit to the bathroom.'

And I left Formal Hall and threw myself into the dark corridors of St Catharine's.

This was a College I'd never been to before, but being endowed with a brain which, as you may or may not have heard, contains as many possible connections as there are stars in the universe, I was able to find my way through it quite easily.

Well, let's say I was lucky enough that the third staircase I got to had a slate that said

Robert Dawes F5

Swiftly, I tiptoed upstairs and followed the corridor. The door to F5 was entirely covered with pictures of rowing-boats, the rowing team, and newspaper cuttings about rowing. This probably meant that it was indeed the lair of Rob Dawes. And this assumption was confirmed by

the thunderous voice of the very man, coming from inside the room. Judging from the absence of audible replies to his sentences, he was either talking on the phone or had become completely mad and was loudly chatting to himself.

'Yes, yes, I know, it's very unexpected! ... But amazing, right? Amazing! ... Yes, in the first boat, I'm in the first boat now! Just like I told you ... Yes, that means I'll be on the Thames next week, rowing against Oxford!' He laughed. 'How many different ways will I have to tell you this? I'm-in-the-first-boat! ... Thank you, thank you ... Me too ... What? Oh, yeah ... Yeah, really mysterious, that virus ... No, don't worry, I'm not catching it, I'm being really careful ... I know, I know ...'

So the illnesses of the fourth and fifth rowers in the first crew had meant that Rob Dawes had been pulled from the reserve crew to race against Oxford.

As I was trying to determine whether he sounded genuinely

surprised or was just an excellent actor and serial poisoner, my ear pressed against the many rowing pictures on the door, a strange sight at the end of the dark corridor caught my eye.

That strange sight was a black silhouette, holding on to one handle of a pirate chest, followed by the pirate chest itself, the second handle of which was held by another black silhouette.

Then this baffling sight disappeared again.

I raced down the corridor, begging my ridiculous shiny shoes to be as silent as possible. If this was the pirate chest of all pirate chests, no wonder it had disappeared from underneath the weeping willow! But who was carrying it?

I caught up with them in the next, tiny stone staircase, where the two silhouettes were painfully negotiating their spirally way down with the pirate chest. Their identities were easily revealed: from where I stood, a dozen steps higher than them, I could clearly make out the angelic blondness of the two stealthy carriers.

Gwendoline and Julius Hawthorne.

I followed them discreetly as they made their huffy and puffy way through another corridor, and then down another staircase. We were underground now, in a creepy, dusty passage spangled with wooden doors: 'Wine Cellar 2', 'Private', 'Archives 1956–1975' …

One single naked lightbulb dangled from the arched ceiling, throwing a gloomy yellow-grey light on to the walls. In the light was dancing the huge shadow of a tiny spider, which was happily walking on the lightbulb in the manner of a fakir. Finally the siblings dropped the chest on to the floor – it made a huge thud which lifted a little sheep of dust into the air – and Gwendoline rubbed her hands together.

'It's damn heavy!' she said.

'At least we didn't bump into anyone,' said Julius.

Gwendoline got a key out of her pocket and opened the door they were facing. I inched closer to it as they got hold of the chest again

and passed the doorstep. The door said, 'Lost Objects.'

I just had time to walk in and dive behind a revoltingly cobwebby coat hanger covered in coats probably dating from the time of Anne Boleyn's early childhood. Gwendoline brushed past me, closed the door, and I was alone with them in this shadowy, sneezingly dusty cellar – alone with them and the pirate chest.

I peeped through a hole in the sleeve of one of the ancient Tudor coats.

'OK,' said Gwendoline. 'Give me the tools.'

Julius opened his backpack and handed his sister a hammer and a long, slim metal bar. She stuck the metal bar just underneath the lock, and started hammering at it as energetically as if the closed chest contained a year's supply of gummy bears.

We waited, and waited, and waited. I would have fallen asleep, if it hadn't been for the deafening racket she was making.

'Want me to take over?' asked Julius after a while.

'Almost … done …' she grumbled between her teeth, still banging at the pirate chest and showering it in pretty sparkles of sweat.

'Would have been easier if you hadn't lost the key,' said Julius.

'Very … funny,' said Gwendoline. 'Haven't … lost it … someone … stole it!'

And finally the lock exploded into splinters of metal and wood, some of which landed dangerously close to my shiny shoes.

'Good job,' said Julius. 'Let's see. Anything missing?'

Gwendoline opened the chest, which groaned as if annoyed to be so rudely awakened (I certainly would have been). They peered into it for a while, moving stuff around.

'Not that I can tell,' murmured Gwendoline. 'No, everything seems to be just as we left it.'

'I told you,' said Julius. 'No one stole that key – you must've lost it somewhere.'

'I was worried about those kids roaming around,' said Gwendoline. 'Your little friends from Goodall.'

'Oh, they're completely harmless,' said Julius. 'I got one of them talking this morning. She told me they suspected that someone was poisoning the team. So I made up a story about seeing Rob Dawes mixing stuff into their food. That should keep them busy for a while.'

I mentally cursed Gemma so abundantly that her unearringed ears must still have been ringing the next morning, though she probably interpreted it as a foreboding of wedding bells with the devious Julius.

'Well,' said Gwendoline, 'until I find the key, let's leave that thing here. We can't hide it anywhere in the Boat House, and we can't leave it outside now that the lock is broken. Let's get what we need from it immediately, and come back for more whenever necessary.'

They crouched down and filled Julius's backpack with things I couldn't see. Then they closed the chest again, pushed it against a wall, covered it with old furs and a Persian rug, and finally left the room, helpfully neglecting to turn the lights off.

As soon as they'd gone, I leapt out of my hiding-place – my lungs as dusty as if I'd been hoovering up the room with my nostrils for the past two hours – and pushed away all the rags that they'd dropped on the chest. Gingerly, I opened it.

It was half-full of bags.

Bags of *powder*.

Blue powder, white powder.

'Well, well, well,' I murmured, 'what can that powder be, then? How about *poison*?'

So I took one, stuck it inside my dress pocket, and put the chest back into place. Then I took some time to congratulate myself.

'Well done, Sesame. This was a good evening. You hadn't planned to go on a mission, but a good supersleuth knows that the unpredictable is always the best ally.'

I shook my own (right) hand with my own (left) hand and merrily prepared to make my way back to the door.

And then the only lightbulb in the cellar gave in with a *ding*!

I didn't panic. Supersleuths don't panic. They embrace the unpredictable. 'Hurrah!' I said to the darkness around me. 'The lights have gone off. This gives me a unique opportunity to use my tiny pen-sized torch.'

My cool godfather Liam, who is a hippie and a punk and sometimes a Goth, but always a good-for-nothing artist, had sent me a while ago a sleuthing package full of useful things. You would know this if you'd read the previous volume of my adventures, like all intelligent people should. Anyway, this package contained, among other things, a pen-sized torch, which I always keep in my pocket. So I got it out and lit my way to the door.

Which was locked.

I didn't panic. Supersleuths don't panic. They embrace the unpredictable.

'Hurrah!' I said to a moth-eaten stuffed weasel with a sparkly tiara on its head next to me. 'The door is locked. This gives me a unique opportunity to use my skeleton key.'

For my cool godfather Liam's package

contained, among other things, a skeleton key, which is a key that can open all doors, or at least a good number of doors.

So I got it out and slid it inside the keyhole, and tweaked and turned and twisted it until the lock went CLICK! and nicely agreed to open the door.

Triumphantly, I pulled the door handle.

Which remained in my hand, problematically not connected to the door, due to its base being entirely eaten up by rust.

I didn't panic. Supersleuths don't panic. They embrace the unpredictable.

'Hurrah!' I said to an ugly painting of a knight on a horse in a field next to me. 'This gives me a unique opportunity to use my phone and call Toby to tell him to get here as fast as possible and open the door from the outside, or else.'

So I got my phone out.

And there was no reception.

Now I can't deny I started panicking a tiny little bit.

VI

'**D**ear parents, I adore you,' I said to Mum and Dad on the way back to Christ's College.

'We adore you too,' said Mum, which proved that she was more than a little bit tipsy.

'It was an über-good idea to give me the hairclip with the flower tonight.'

'I'm sure it was, my love.'

'It saved my life.'

'I'm sure it did, my love.'

They stumbled into Christ's, threw loud hellos to the Night Porters, and danced around First Court to our front door.

'Looks like they had a good evening,' said Tod the Porter to me as I was bidding goodnight to him and Don.

'Yep,' I said. 'They didn't even notice I was gone for an hour, almost buried alive, and would have died a long and hungry death had it not been for a metal hairclip I managed to use as a door handle to free myself from a room of Lost Objects containing a pirate chest full of illegal poison.'

'So many funny stories in that little head,' said Don, shuffling my hair.

I hugged them both, leaving a vast amount of cobwebs and dust on their uniforms, and skipped home where a concerto in snore major

was already emanating from the parental bedroom. I emptied my pocket on the table, found my phone, and texted Gemma quickly:

> Julius & Gwen guilty. Poison in St Cats. Rob not guilty. Do not accept marriage proposal from JH. He's a filthy criminal and will be hanged high and short, leaving you widowed and publicly shamed xx

Then I realised I was about to collapse with exhaustion, and almost did, but Peter Mortimer started licking my ankles with a tongue that was slightly more unpleasant than a cheesegrater, so I moved to bed and fell instantly asleep.

'Bonjour, hungover parents! How's the head?'

'We are not at all hungover,' said Mum curtly, spreading jam on her toast. Dad was idly pretending to read the *Telegraph*. 'We remember everything that happened yesterday evening.'

Both of them were sporting impressively dark half-circles under their eyes, making them look like a couple of giant cuddly raccoons.

'Like when I was away for an hour at the end of the dinner?'

'Very funny,' said Dad. 'Here's your porridge. Sugar? Honey?'

And he pushed a jar of honey towards me, as well as an open bag of ...

I froze.

'That's not sugar,' I said.

They didn't reply, so I said more loudly, 'That's not sugar.'

'What isn't, my dear?' asked Mum, who was now reading the centrepiece of the *Telegraph* which Dad had shared with her.

'That bag. Bad powder. Not sugar,' I stammered, having suddenly lost the ability to use verbs.

'Yes, it is,' said Mum, stirring a spoonful of the substance into her cup of coffee, and then drinking it.

'No no, no no no, no no, no no,' I choked. 'Don't drink it!'

'It's my second cup,' said Mum, laughing. 'What's wrong with you, Sophie?'

'It's not sugar,' I said. 'It's a bag of ... something ... which I left here on the table yesterday. By mistake.'

Mum rolled her eyes, and tucked into her newspaper again.

Being faced with two *Telegraph*-shaped walls, I looked at the transparent plastic bag. Sure enough, there was writing on it, small enough that I hadn't noticed it the night before. It said

FINE WHITE SUGAR (500g).

'But it can't be,' I murmured. 'It makes no sense. Why hide sugar in a pirate chest?'

'What are you mumbling in your beard?' inquired Dad from behind the *Telegraph* wall.

'Are you feeling well?' I asked. 'No nausea?'

'Seriously, Sophie,' said Dad, 'we're not hungover at all. It was just a little bit of wine.'

'Any rumbling and fizzling in your stomach? Any urgent urges to be violently sick?'

'Really, Sophie, you are infernal,' said Mum. 'We don't need to hear such disgusting things at the breakfast table. Finish your porridge, you're going to be late for school.'

And when I left the house, half an hour later, neither Mum nor Dad was projectile-vomiting into the purple curtains.

It was incomprehensible.

While all the other kids were at school doing algebra, Gemma, Toby, and I were on a small motorboat on the river in Ely.

'Sometimes I love being your sidekick, Sesame,' said Toby.

The motorboat was steered by Gwendoline, who was shouting orders at the top of her voice to the University rowing-boat next to us. The

boat was coxed by Will, who was adding more orders to the wild rumpus. It sounded like this:

'Come on, boys! Oxford won't be waiting for you to catch up at the first corner!'

'And push for ten! One! Two! Three! ...'

'Up one, down one!'

'Going up to thirty-eight now! Thirty-six at the moment!'

I was trying quite hard not to stare at the boat, as I had to look at Gwendoline's hands and pretend to be fabulously stupid, but it wasn't an easy task.

'Don't forget we're on a mission,' I whispered to Gemma and Toby. 'We have to figure out why Gwen and Julius are hiding bags of sugar in that chest.'

'Maybe it wasn't just sugar,' said Toby, looking into the screen of his camera. 'Maybe the bag you took was sugar, but the rest was poison.'

'Maybe,' I admitted.

'You're both mental,' snapped Gemma. 'There's no reason why Julius and Gwendoline would poison their own team. I'm sure there's a

perfectly rational explanation to this pirate chest mystery. It's obviously Rob – he poisoned enough people to get into the first crew, that's all.'

'Gemma, I've already told you it's not him. Julius made that up after you unequivocally explained to him everything about our mission.'

'I barely said anything!' protested Gemma. 'I was just trying to make conversation. And anyway, maybe Julius's right, but he doesn't know it. It's Rob, I'm sure.'

We passed under a bridge, and the farts and hiccoughs of the motorboat's engine scared a lazy-looking heron, which flew away into the distance with an expression of profound disgust on its face.

'Or maybe it's as everyone always suspected,' said Toby. 'A virus, just a virus.'

'But my mum said it was a man-made one,' I objected.

'Precisely,' said Gemma triumphantly. 'Gwendoline would never be able to make a virus like that. She did Fine Art at Oxford. She isn't a scientist.'

'Hey, that's a good point,' I muttered. 'Ask Gwendoline what the other rowers on the team do.'

Gemma cleared her throat and switched to goody-goody mode. 'Gwendoline? Sorry to bother you – we're just thinking that for the article, we'd like to indicate what each of the rowers studies at University. Would you be able to tell us?'

'Sure,' said Gwendoline, her eyes still riveted to the rowing-boat next to us. 'Alex at Bow does English. Salman and Dan are both Engineers. Rob does Medieval History. Danny does Physics, and so does Andrew, I think ... Then there's Joe, an Astronomer. And at Stroke, Gary, who's a Medic. As for Wally,' she laughed, 'he studies frogs for his doctorate.'

'Frogs!' exclaimed Toby. 'Wicked! I love Wally more and more. I mean, Will.'

'Gary's a Medicine student,' I murmured. 'This could be our man.'

'Gwendoline?' asked Gemma again. 'Has Gary been pulled from the reserve crew?'

'Nope,' she said, 'he's always been in the First crew. He's …'

But she suddenly stopped talking, and cut the engine. Next to us, the rowers had slowed down considerably.

'What's going on, boys?' she shouted. 'Why are you losing speed?'

'Gary's got a problem,' replied Will from the cox's seat.

'What's wrong, Gary?' asked Gwendoline.

And just as I heard the CLICK! of Toby's camera near my ear, Gary leant to his right over the edge of the boat, and emptied the (colourful) contents of his stomach into the river.

'Well,' said Toby to lighten up the atmosphere, 'at least the fish got some extra food for tea.'

But no one seemed to have switched on their sense of humour, unfortunately, so the three of us sat down under a nearby tree and waited as the whole crew disembarked, and dragged a semi-comatose and very white Gary on to the grass. They rowed back as a seven, leaving Gary with us on the motorboat.

'Mystery reactivated,' I said. 'There's no reason why Rob should have poisoned someone else – he's already on the crew. So it can't be him. It could be the next guy they'll pull in from the reserve boat, though.'

'Or,' said Gemma, 'it could simply be A Bug! Maybe there's no mystery at all, Sesame.'

'If it's A Bug,' said Toby, 'we've definitely caught it, having spent twenty minutes with Gary on that tiny boat.'

UR. BleuRGh...

The boys were in the changing-rooms, and Gwendoline disappeared into the Boat House. Will walked down towards us, looking very concerned.

'Please don't publish this article before the race,' he said. 'We can't let Oxford know that we're six men down.'

'Don't worry,' said Gemma in a professional tone, 'we know our responsibilities.'

We walked back to the Boat House. Inside, Rob Dawes came to us with a box of chocolates.

'Want some, kids?' he said. 'If you're still hungry after all this ...'

We were indeed, and helped ourselves copiously. While Gemma was asking him some innocent questions, and while Toby was taking pictures, I spotted Gwendoline's reflection in a darkened window.

She was in the kitchenette, at the end of a short corridor, half-hidden from everyone's sight.

I crept up the corridor and looked.

And what I saw made me open up my mouth as wide as Peter Mortimer's when he's about to give a squirrel the bite of death.

For Gwendoline Hawthorne was scooping blue powder from a white bucket into a large jug of juice, and mixing, and mixing, and mixing.

'It's you!' I shouted, pointing at her. 'You're the poisoner!'

'What?' she exclaimed, turning to me. 'What's that about? Oh, it's you. I didn't know you could even talk.'

'Oh, yes, I can,' I sniggered. 'I can talk very well, and also deduce things from what I see. You're slowly poisoning your own team so Oxford can win. Pathetic!'

She burst out laughing. 'That's the most absurd thing I've ever heard,' she said.

'I know where you hide your powder,' I said. 'I don't know how you made that virus, but I know where it is now – in the cellars of St Catharine's College!'

She suddenly went as white as Toby's frog's belly. 'I don't know what you're talking about. But I suggest you and your friends get out of here right now. Wally!'

'Yes?' said Will, who was walking up to us with Gemma and Toby.

'Send the baby journalists home right now.'

'Erm … okey-doke,' said Will, 'but why?'

'Why?' I repeated. 'Because she wants some peace and quiet to poison the whole team with that virus!'

There was a long, very long silence, so long that I wondered if I'd accidentally hit the 'pause' button of Life.

But then Will murmured, 'I'm not sure I understand.'

'It's quite simple,' said Gwendoline. 'This ridiculous child is accusing me of trying to poison everyone.'

'Poison? Why poison?' laughed Will, looking at me. 'It's a virus that people are getting, you know, not poison.'

'It *is* a virus,' I said, 'but a man-made one. Someone is deliberately giving it to the rowers. And that someone is her, with the help of her brother.'

'You're an idiot,' said Gwendoline. 'This, my dear, is a protein shake, which I make every day for the guys in the crew.'

Toby and Gemma slapped their foreheads, and I slouched a little. Gwendoline had poured

96

herself a glass of the weird mixture, and downed it in one.

'See? I'm not throwing up any time soon. Because it's just extra protein to make them stronger. Maybe you'll learn that at school some day. In the meantime, get out of here. Wally, drive them home. I've had enough of those kids, we're not taking them back in the van.'

So we got out of there, under the sarcastic glances of the seven remaining boys, and Will's concerned look.

'Sorry about that,' he said to us as we squeezed into his tiny, rusty car. 'It's not a good time to get people on the crew angry. We're all a bit stressed about all the losses. That bug ... It's ruining our chances, you know. And for most of the guys on the team, it's the opportunity of a lifetime. They've been dreaming of the Boat Race for years.'

'But Will,' I said, 'you've got to believe us, there's something dodgy about that bug. We really think someone is feeding it to the rowers. Maybe someone who's trying to get into the

97

first crew, we don't know, but ...'

Will was shaking from head to foot. 'It's a horrible thought,' he said. 'I don't know what makes you think that, but I'm sure you're wrong – it's just a bug, probably in the river. Have some antibacterial gel, by the way. Wouldn't want you to fall ill too. What a dreadful epidemic.'

He pointed at the tube of gel in the glove compartment, and we helped ourselves.

'But don't you find it weird that Gwendoline is from Oxford and coaching the Cambridge team?' I asked.

'Not at all,' he said, 'the Hawthornes have lived in Cambridge for generations. Gwen went to Oxford because she wanted to do Fine Art, which you can't do in Cambridge. Seriously, kids, don't look any further. Everyone wants us to win – everyone except the river and the bug in it.'

He dropped us off in the city centre in Cambridge, and we had to admit it had been another very bad day for sleuthing.

I gloomily passed by the gate of Christ's

College. It was very hot, I thought, even though it was apparently raining. And I was very tired, even though it was only five o'clock. The river air, probably.

'Good evening, Sophie.'

'Evening, parents.'

'How was the outing? How's the article going?'

'Not great.'

'You're not very chatty tonight.'

'No.'

That's when I fell on to the armrest of the armchair, bounced off it, landed on the floor, was even more colourfully sick than Gary, and then all I remember is █████████████

██████████████████████████

VII

'**E**nough, Mother! A week of carrots is enough for anyone. I am not a bunny! *Je ne suis pas un* bunny! *No soy un* bunny! I don't want to see or smell another carrot in my life. I wish carrots would disappear from the surface of the planet. In fact they probably are disappearing, since you're feeding them all to me.'

'The problem with Sophie is that she's a dramatic little Sarah Bernhardt,' sighed Mum. 'Eat your carrot puree.'

'I'm warning you, if I do end up turning into a rabbit, I'll leave perfectly round little turds everywhere in the house. Everywhere. That'll teach you.'

'Eat your carrot puree.'

'Bring me a rare, juicy, sinewy leg of lamb.'

'Eat this and then you can have a banana.'

'How about food for humans? I demand chicken korma and blackberry crumble.'

'Not until you are cured.'

'I am cured! I haven't thrown up in fifteen hours and twelve minutes. Thirteen now. Can I go to school?'

'No. Eat.'

I yawned, and she took advantage of the open mouth to thrust an enormous spoonful of the disgusting orange paste into it.

'You're shuch a bad nurshe,' I shpluttered. 'Dad ish a mushch better nurshe than you. He'sh all shweet and caring and he shtrokes my head. Where ish he?'

'At shursh,' said Mum, 'I mean church. Eat your carrots, and then shleep. I mean sleep. I'm going to work; have a nice day.'

She walked out, and I sighed. It was Friday. Toby, Gemma and I had been out of action for a whole week, and the Boat Race was tomorrow.

In sickness or in health, there was no way I'd

let the serial poisoner get away with it.

As soon as Mum had left the house, I got out my phone and went click-click-click-call.

'Hello-hello?' said Gemma's voice at the other end of the line. 'Who's the lucky person who's got the honour of talking to me?'

'Sesame,' I said. 'But I think you'll find *you*'ve got the honour of talking to *me*.'

'Hello, Sess! How long since you last threw up?'

'Fifteen hours and twenty-one minutes. You?'

'Twelve hours and two minutes.'

'We're basically cured.'

'That's what I keep telling my parents, but they won't stop feeding me white rice.'

'I'd kill for white rice! I've had carrot puree thrust down my throat for the past five days in the manner of a turkey being fattened up for Christmas.'

'I'd kill for carrot puree!'

102

said Gemma. 'I've eaten so much rice these past five days that I've become at least half-Chinese.'

'You were already half-Chinese,' I pointed out.

'I must admit that that is true, admittedly,' she admitted. 'Anyway, I've just talked to Toby. He hasn't thrown up in almost twenty-two hours! And he's really fed up with eating nothing but hard-boiled eggs. He's had so many in the past five days that he's collected enough bits of shell to make a giant mosaic covering a whole wall of his bedroom.'

I tut-tutted. '*Ergo*, we are not at all sick any more. We have to meet up and continue the investigation.'

'Yes. But how can I get out of Waterbeach?'

Waterbeach is where Gemma lives, in what looks like a many-turretted castle. It's got no beach, however, and the only water

is that which falls from the sky every time you forget your umbrella. It's at least 25 minutes by car, which makes it one of the furthest places from Cambridge I've ever been to. Well, apart from Paris when I was in Mum's belly, and I couldn't see the Eiffel Tower very well through her skin and dress, so I slept most of the time.

'Tell your parents to drive you. Just say that the three of us are meeting up at Toby's to recover all together and catch up on homework,' I said. 'And don't forget to call Toby to tell him. I'll be there in ten mins. Running out of credit! See you la—'

And then the phone went silent, my five pounds of monthly phone credit having been eaten up by that greedy Gemma.

I leapt out of bed and reached under my desk for my faithful rollerskates, which looked extremely bored, having not been used for a week. Thankfully the wheels still seemed to remember how to roll around their little axles. I slid down the big tree and escaped through the back door.

And then I whooshed through town, perhaps a little bit more wobblily than usual, but readier than ever for some serious supersleuthing.

'That is one splendid eggshell mosaic, Toby,' I congratulated him. 'Three piglets tripping over marbles in a jungle. How original.'

'It's not three piglets tripping over marbles in a jungle, it's you, me and Gemma cycling, skating and scooting through Cambridge.'

'Oh. I see. Well, it's very impressionistic. Or something-istic, at least. I think you've launched a completely new type of art. It's properly Tobyfying.'

'Thank you,' said the artist. 'Ah, Gemma's here!'

And indeed, Gemma, freshly disembarked from her mum's car, was walking up the alley to Toby's house. Toby's house, due to his parents being the caretaker and the cook at Goodall, is right behind Goodall, near the sports field. From his bedroom window we could see our class playing mixed netball. Mr Halitosis, hopping among them breathlessly like an asthmatic

kangaroo, was shouting, 'Come on, come on, a bit more energy! I feel like I'm watching a whole team of Sophie Seades!'

'I'm super honoured that Halitosis thinks of me even when I'm not there,' I said. 'Right, team: we've still got a mystery to solve. Who's poisoning everyone? And what's in Gwendoline's pirate chest?'

'I've had some time to think about it while painting eggshells,' said Toby. 'I think Rob is the one who's doing it.'

'It makes no sense,' I said. 'He's already on the team.'

'I know. But listen. I have a hypotenuse.'

'Hypothesis,' I rectified. 'Unless you're a right-angled triangle.'

'Shut it, Sesame. So – Rob designs a little virus with the help of someone. He puts it in chocolates, which he gives to people on the team until he can get in. But then he forgets which chocolates have the viruses, and keeps giving them to people accidentally. Remember those chocolates he gave us the other day?

They're the ones that were full of viruses.'

I whistled. 'I'd forgotten about those chocolates. The virus could have been in there, it's true.'

'See,' said Toby, 'my hypothermia was completely right.'

'Hypothesis. But no, I'm afraid it can't be right, Toby. If someone's clever enough to think up a plan like that, they're not going to forget where they've put the deadly bug. But of course, Rob could well have another reason to want to poison everyone – a reason that's got nothing to do with being on the first crew.'

'Maybe he's an evil mastermind,' suggested Gemma, 'just doing it for fun and out of pure malevolence. Or an international terrorist employed by Lapland to destroy Cambridge.'

'Yes. Somehow, I'm not convinced.'

'Well, do you have another hypochondria?' asked Toby.

'Hypothesis. Yes, I do. I think there's something we haven't yet thought about. And to find out what it is, we have to go back to the

Boat House and investigate.'

So we escaped through the kitchen window, having checked that Mr and Mrs Appleyard were busy doing something else (she was telling him that one and a half buckets of goose fat and six packs of butter was quite enough fat for today's school lunch). Since Gemma didn't have her scooter with her, she sat on the back of Toby's bike, and after he'd finished complaining about how heavy she was (heavier than a blue whale who's swallowed an elephant who's pregnant with twins, apparently), we crossed town and stopped at the University Boat House.

Which was, unsurprisingly, locked and empty. So close to the race, the team must be spending most of the day in Ely, rowing on the river and doing gym sessions to wind down before eating kilos of pasta.

'They've left the changing-room window open again!' I said as we reached the little balcony, having climbed up the wooden beam.

We slithered inside, and immediately switched to supersleuth-and-sidekicks mode.

My supersleuth radar, which is a sort of sixth sense you get when the stellar connections in your brain are particularly good at detecting criminal action, was on full blare.

'Here are Rob's chocolates!' called Gemma from the other side of the changing-rooms. She read the label on the box. '"An assortment of drop-dead delicious fondants and lip-lickingly luscious ganaches."'

'Drop-dead, I bet,' Toby sniggered.

'Bag them all,' I said. 'We'll analyse them later.'

'I don't have a bag,' remarked Gemma.

We looked everywhere for an appropriate bag, but of one there was no sign.

'Just put them in that silly woolly hat,' I said, pointing at the red-and-white hat we'd seen last time, and which was lying under a bench.

Toby dived under the bench to pick it up. 'It's full,' he said.

'Of what? Lice? Dandruff? Brains? It's funny, it reminds me of—'

'Oh wow,' he interrupted, looking inside it.

109

'Not … quite. Look at that.'

And he emptied it on the floor.

And it went *cling-a-ling*!

Ding-a-ding-a-cling-a-ling!

And showered us and the room with light.

Glitters.

Glimmers.

Shimmers.

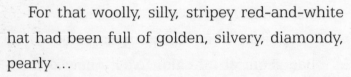

For that woolly, silly, stripey red-and-white hat had been full of golden, silvery, diamondy, pearly …

'*Jewellery!*' gasped Gemma. 'Geez! Since when has that been here?'

'Since when do you say "geez"?' asked Toby.

'The thieves,' I whispered. 'Gemz – the thieves that the pirate was talking about!'

'What thieves?'

'The zieves!'

'Ah, yes, the zieves. What about them?'

'They're here! In the Boat House! Stealing from barges, burgling them! All that in order to …'

All the neurons in my brain lined themselves

up into a nice little hypothermia. I mean, hypothesis.

'... in order to pay for the poison! Yes, that's it! Since they can't make it themselves, they're paying for someone else to make it for them!'

'Who?' asked Toby. 'Rob?'

'No,' I said. 'Not Rob. Julius and Gwendoline Hawthorne.'

'Ah, no!' protested Gemma. 'Stop it with that stupid idea. You humiliated us enough last time. How many times will I need to tell you? They've got nothing to do with that!'

'I have clues, this time,' I said. 'Remember what the pirate told me? That the silhouette of the thief that they'd seen was a short, small man. Why short and small? Because he's eleven years old! Gwen sends him stealing from the barges. It can't possibly have been Rob – he's huge.'

'I refuse to believe it,' said Gemma. 'They want Cambridge to win. They wouldn't poison anyone.'

'Refuse to believe it all you like,' I said, 'as long as you lend me your phone. I need to call Jeremy and I've run out of credit.'

She agreed reluctantly, and I dialled Susie's number.

'Hello?' said Jeremy's voice on the other end of the line.

'Hello, boss. Sesame Seade speaking.'

'What's up, Sess?'

'I've found enough clues to frame Gwendoline Hawthorne and her brother Julius.'

'Excellent news. Can you write it all down in an email?'

'No, you have to come over. I'm at the University Boat House.'

'I can't possibly. I've got an essay crisis. And my foot's hurting a bit, and also I'm going out for coffee with some girl later ...'

'Come here immediately or I'm handing in my notice.'

'I'll be with you in five minutes.'

I hung up and turned to the sidekicks. 'Right, let's go and wait for him outside.'

So we wormed our way out through the window, climbed over the balcony, slid down the wooden beam, and jumped to the grou—

'Zis time I've GOT you!'

And as we kicked the air to try to escape the mighty clutch, we heard the terrible, awful, horrible, ignoble, not-good-news-at-all noise of a rain of jewellery on the floor.

And behind us, the voice of the French pirate:

'You see, Patricia? What did I tell you! It's zem! It's ZEM! ZEY ARE ZE ZIEVES!'

VIII

'OK,' I said, 'I know what it looks like. But it's a hilarious misunderstanding. Just put us down on the floor and we'll explain, and you'll laugh your head off.'

Marcel put us down on the floor and said, 'I'm not laughing yet!'

'Let me explain. It's really funny, because you think we've just stolen all this jewellery.'

'Very funny indeed,' growled Patricia.

'But in fact we haven't. We absolutely haven't.'

'You have,' said Marcel. 'Well, in fact, *you* have!' he added, pointing at Toby.

'Me?' exclaimed Toby.

'We've seen you many times! We saw you

again on Monday night!' thundered Marcel. 'Jumping away from Fran's barge, having stolen her little gold chain with ze little boat charm on it!'

'She told us she'd been burgled the next morning,' said Patricia. 'And we put two and two together. It was you we saw running away from the barge!'

'It can't have been,' I said, 'because Toby, Gemma and I have been massively sick for the past week. We've been throwing up every two minutes in the manner of volcanoes erupting.'

'No, I'm almost certain it was him,' said Patricia decidedly. 'Short, brown-haired like that ... Are you going to pretend it was a coincidence again?'

'Yes,' I said.

'Complete coincidence, as it happens.'

'And zat?' boomed Marcel. 'Zat's a coincidence, perhaps?'

He'd scooped up the pile of jewellery from the floor, and was dangling in front of our eyes a little gold chain with a little boat charm attached to it.

'Yes,' I said. 'Funny coincidence, I know.'

'We're taking you to ze police,' said Marcel.

'Yes,' I said, 'I was worried you might.'

Gemma and Toby, meanwhile, were absolutely petrified. What is the point, I ask you, of sidekicks who don't kick people's sides when sides are in need of kicking? But Toby was staring longingly at the river like a fish that's just been fished and thrown into a fishing basket, and Gemma was staring forcefully at the pile of jewels as if plunged into a deep hypnotic state.

'Seriously,' I said, 'you've got the absolutely innocent zieves here. We were indeed zieving, but zieving from the zieves. I'm not at all even a tiny bit of a zief. I'm a supersleuth: a world-

famous supersleuth on skates. I've got such a strong sense of justice that I'd arrest my own mother. Thinking about it, I *have* arrested my own mother.'

While talking, I was kicking the sides of my sidekicks, hoping to summon some sort of response, but they were still being as reactive as a pair of hibernating marmots.

'My friend is coming with her car to take you to the police station!' announced Patricia, putting her mobile phone back into her pocket. 'You'll have to explain to them how you thieved from the actual thieves. I'm sure they'll be very interested. And also interested to hear about where the rest of the jewellery is. From what I can tell, this is only what's been gathered in the past two weeks! Where's the watch that you stole a month ago from my barge?'

'I know not,' I admitted politely, 'for never in my life have I laid eyes on it.'

'I'm sure they'll make you talk,' said Patricia.

'I wish they'd make Toby and Gemma talk,' I said. 'I'm tired of doing all the talking. Toby!

Gemma! Anything you'd like to say in our defence?'

'Earrings,' said Gemma.

'Frogs,' said Toby.

'Bother,' I said, 'their brains appear to have disappeared.'

'Earrings,' insisted Gemma. 'My earrings. There!'

So I looked at what she was looking at, and indeed and undeniably, those were her earrings, emerging from the pile of jewellery that Marcel was still holding.

'Oh, that's where they were!' I said. 'You lost them in the Boat House, and then the zief just had to bend down and pick them up. He must have been pretty chuffed.'

'Can I have them back, please?' asked Gemma. 'They're mine.'

'No,' said the pirate. 'Ah, Patricia's friend is coming! Oh, no, it's not Patricia's friend, it's a tramp.'

It wasn't a tramp, in fact; it was Jeremy being his usual stylish self, that is to say, dressed in

clothes older than my dad's jokes.

'Jeremy!' I greeted him. 'So nice to see you. Pray tell this gentleman I'm not a zief.'

'She isn't a zief,' said Jeremy obligingly. 'What's a zief?' he added, looking at me.

'Someone who steals zings!' said Marcel. 'And who are you? Zeir zief-in-chief?'

'No,' said Jeremy, 'I'm a student at Gonville & Caius.'

'You'll have to explain zat to the police,' said the pirate. 'We're taking ze kids zere, and we'll happily take you along.'

Jeremy sighed. 'Ah. That's not entirely ideal, as I need to finish an essay for yesterday morning and I haven't started thinking about it yet.'

'You'll zink about it at ze police station,' suggested Marcel.

'I would, but I can't for the life of me remember what the question is. Sesame, can you please explain what's going on?'

'Yes,' I said. 'We went into the Boat House to steal Rob Dawes's chocolates which we thought were poisonous. But then we found

a woolly hat full of stolen jewellery and stole that instead. We were then caught on our way out by Monsieur Marcel here, who is under the wrong but understandable impression that we are the notorious barge-burgling zieves who've been spreading chaos and desolation among the river-dwellers of late.'

'I see,' said Jeremy. 'Well, not really.'

That's when the University Team's van from Ely arrived. Will got off first, and looked immediately terrified.

'Hey, what's going on?' he said, drawing closer to us. 'What are you doing here, kids?'

'We've just intercepted these children leaving the Boat House with a bag of jewellery that we know has been stolen from local barges over the past few weeks,' explained Patricia. 'We're taking them to the police station.'

Gwen, from the doorstep of the Boat House, called, 'What's the matter, Wally? What are the crazy kids doing here *again*?'

'Nothing,' replied Will, 'I'm dealing with it! Do the debrie ing without me!'

And Gwendoline and the rowers disappeared into the Boat House. Will turned to Marcel and Patricia again. 'Are you sure it's them?' he asked hesitantly.

'It's seriously not us at all,' I said, 'it's Gwendoline. Or Rob. Or Julius, or someone. But not us.'

Will addressed a reassuring smile to me. 'Listen,' he said to our kidnappers, 'I really don't think these kids have anything to do with this. They're just would-be-journalists. Let me

drive you to the police station and we'll talk about it there, OK? But leave the children here. I'm pretty sure it's not their fault. And anyway, they're too young to be arrested.'

'*He*'s not too young,' objected Marcel, pointing at Jeremy.

'Well, we'll take him along,' said Will. 'Let's go.'

Marcel seemed reluctant, but then he said, 'OK, zen. Patricia, call your friend and tell her we don't need her any more. You're coming with us,' he said to Jeremy. 'As for you, children …' he pointed a menacing finger at our face, 'if I see you again …'

And the three little dots were more terrifying than any actual threat could ever be.

'I'm so glad I came,' moaned Jeremy, rolling his eyes. 'Sesame, you can say goodbye to your salary this month.'

I felt bad, but it's not as if he ever pays me anyway. Marcel and Jeremy squeezed into Will's car and Will drove off, leaving Toby, Gemma, Patricia, the woolly hat and me on the river bank.

'Sesame,' said Toby, 'now they're gone, can I just tell you something that's just struck me as just a little bit strange?'

'What?'

'While you were busy defending us, I was looking at another frog, and really, I mean really, the frogs around here are very, very fast.'

When Toby's got something he wants to do, you have to let him do it. You have to let him do it because otherwise he'll say every two minutes, 'Let me do it,' and sing it to the tune of famous nursery rhymes, which is incredibly annoying, especially as he learnt the trick from me.

'OK, Toby!' I exploded. 'Organise that frog race if you really want to. It's fine.'

'Yippee! You'll see, it will be grand.'

We were back at Toby's house and waiting to hear from Jeremy about the cosiness of the police station and the friendliness of the police officers. But he hadn't texted yet, which didn't bode particularly well, unless he was busy carving his essay on the walls of his

cells with his own fingernails.

'There we go,' said Toby, 'it's all ready. Come and watch!'

He took us to the bathroom, where he'd filled the bath with cold water. In little jugs on one end of the bath were his two frogs.

'The green one is the one I found near the University Boat House,' he said. 'The brownish one I caught in the pond behind the school. Look at that.'

He turned the two jugs over, and the frogs leapt into the water in a joyous splish-splash. And then they started to swim around.

Well, the brownish one swam around. The

green one was darting to and fro so fast it can't possibly have been called swimming.

'Calm it down,' I said, 'or it'll go faster than light and create a black hole in your bath tub that will swallow up the entire Earth, and I want to know the end of this story before that can happen.'

'That's what I mean,' said Toby. 'It's hugely fast.'

'So what?'

'So,' said Toby, 'I was just wondering if they're hugely fast because of something they're eating around the University Boat House.'

And suddenly all the neurons in my brain

 started to whisper things to one another.

Whisper whisper, blah-di-blah, and don't you think, and maybe it could be, and possibly, and why not this, oh, surely not, but perhaps yes, and suddenly all the cogs slotted into place and ...

'GENIUS! Toby, you're a GENIUS!'

'I know,' he said modestly.

'This is EXACTLY what we've ALL been waiting for!'

'I know,' he said. 'Once we've figured out what it is that makes the frogs so fast, all the frog collectors in the world will want it. We'll be rich!'

I froze.

'Toby. It's not just about frogs.'

'Isn't it? What's it about, then?'

I looked at Gemma. 'Tell him, Gemz.'

'Sure,' she said. 'It's about ... Well ... Why don't *you* tell us, Sesame?'

'What?' I groaned. 'You haven't guessed?

126

Sometimes I despair of having such short-sighted sidekicks. OK, so – frogs are faster around the Boat House. What's in the water there in high concentrations? The water from the Boat House, of course – the sewers lead there.'

'That's disgusting,' said Gemma. 'The frogs are drinking sewer water?'

'Probably not coming from the toilet, but the water coming from the kitchens, certainly.'

'And?'

'And what if this water coming from the kitchen is loaded with something that makes people stronger? That makes people *faster*?'

Gemma's jaw dropped. 'Drugs?'

'Yes. Some kind of dope. Some kind of drug that makes the rowers more efficient. Some kind of drug that someone inside the Boat House is giving them – mixing into their food.'

'But that's forbidden,' objected Toby.

'Quite. Very forbidden. So this person has to be very discreet. So discreet, in fact, that no one knows, apart from this person, that this is

happening. Even the rowers don't know that they're being drugged. So the stocks of dope have to be hidden in a safe place, not in the Boat House, but in …'

'… the pirate chest!' whispered Gemma.

'And the drug has to be mixed to something else, something that makes it easy to give to the rowers without them noticing, such as …'

'… the protein shake!' whispered Toby.

'And so that the taste isn't too weird, that drug has to be mixed with a vast amount of …'

'… fine white sugar,' whispered Gemma.

'And the people who are doing it are clearly, uncontroversially and undeniably …'

'Gwendoline and Julius Hawthorne,' whispered Toby.

'Yes. Gwendoline and Julius Hawthorne, carrying their pirate chest around St Cat's cellars, which is where they found it in the first place. Julius who's been spotted by the pirates jumping from barge to barge, stealing jewels … to pay for the drugs! And Gwendoline who mixes drugs into the protein shakes …'

We all looked at each other. Everything was silent. Even the frogs had stopped swimming and were exchanging meaningful glances over the water with their huge, bulbous eyes.

'But there's just one thing I don't understand,' said Toby after a while. 'I thought we were looking for a serial poisoner?'

IX

'Well, we were,' I admitted. 'But … maybe we're not any more. Maybe it's just a virus, as we always said. Anyway, we've got bigger fry to fish now. We need to decide what we're going to do about this.'

'Denounce them to the police,' said Toby.

'But then the Boat Race will be cancelled!' moaned Gemma. 'And what if you're wrong, Sesame? What if there's something else we haven't thought about? You could kiss goodbye to your supersleuth career if you claimed that and it wasn't true!'

'Gemma's right,' I said. 'We need to get someone on our side first, and fact-check. We need to find someone nice. Someone who'd

understand. Someone who could check things for us. Someone who knows how it works.'

'Jeremy?' suggested Toby.

'Jeremy still isn't calling, so we can assume that he's probably being kept in jail or something.'

'How about Wally?' said Toby. 'Or Will, rather. He's nice.'

'Yes! Good idea. I'll go and see him now.'

'What? It's almost four o'clock! Your parents will want you back at some point,' said Toby. 'Especially as they don't even know you've gone.'

'Zounds! I'd forgotten about them. How vexing. Listen – why don't you tell your parents that we're all staying over at yours tonight, to talk about how rubbish it is to be ill and to catch up on our homework. I'll call my parents from your phone and tell them I'm sleeping at yours. Then I'll leave, and if your parents ask where I am, just stuff the guest bed with pillows and say that I've fallen asleep.'

'Okeydoke,' said Toby. 'Stay in touch!'

I quickly called my parents and explained. They were furious that I'd gone without telling them, and refused to let me sleep over. I insisted. They refused again. I insisted again. They refused again. I insisted a bit more. They accepted.

So then I squeezed my feet into my purple rollerskates, and skated through town to find Will's room at Homerton College.

Will was in his room when I knocked. He looked like he needed a good camomile tea and a long night's sleep. He also looked like I was the last person in the world he wanted to see, apart perhaps from Death itself with his mighty scythe.

'Hey,' I said. 'Can I come in?'

'What are you doing here, Sesame?'

'I need your help.'

'I'm leaving with the team in half an hour. We're spending the night in London before the race tomorrow morning.'

'I won't need more than half an hour.'

He let me in. His room was full of pictures

of the rowing team, and of posters of brightly coloured tropical frogs. I sat down on his desk chair. On his desk was a draft of his thesis, entitled 'Lipophilic alkaloid in the *Phyllobates Terribilis*: A study of toxicity for human epiderm.'

'That sounds crazy complicated,' I small-talked.

'It's just jargon,' said Will. 'It means I'm studying the ways in which these little tropical frogs produce a very active toxin – a sort of poison, if you will – which comes directly from their skin, and can penetrate human skin too. It can be very dangerous – if you so much as touch them, you could die.'

'Wicked. You'll have to talk to my friend Toby. He'd be very interested. He loves frogs. He's got two.'

Will laughed, 'I've got over thirty at the lab. And I had to buy some more recently.'

'You'll have to give Toby a tour of your lab!' I exclaimed. 'Anyway, back to business. What

happened at the police station? Is Jeremy being kept in a dark dungeon and having to catch his own cockroaches for dinner?'

'No,' sighed Will. 'Unfortunately, Jeremy and Marcel fell extremely sick almost as soon as we got to the police station. They had to be taken to the doctor's urgently. Well, you know what it's like, you had the bug for a week.'

'Oh, poor Jeremy. That explains why he wasn't calling me. What did the police say?'

'Well, Marcel and Jeremy were sick literally on the doorstep of the police station, so we didn't even have time to go in and talk to the police. And I didn't know anything about this affair, so ... we'll see about that after the Boat Race, when they've both recovered.'

'What happened to the jewellery?'

'Oh, I have it here,' said Will. 'I'll keep it until they're both better and we can go to the police again.'

'OK. Don't give it back to Julius and Gwendoline,' I advised.

'Julius and Gwendoline? What do you mean?'

'That they're the ones who stole the jewellery. To pay for dope.'

'To pay for what?' laughed Will.

'They're mixing drugs into the crew's food. Performance-enhancing drugs. All the rowers on the team are doped.'

And I explained everything: the pirate chest, the night at St Cat's, the barge people's jewellery being stolen, the frogs.

Will was silent as a stone. Then he said, 'That's very serious. Very, very serious, Sesame.'

'I know,' I said. 'What shall we do? We'll have to denounce them to the police and cancel the race, surely.'

He started shaking like a washing-machine. 'Let's ... let's not be too hasty. This race means a lot to all of us, you know.'

'Yes, but it's cheating. It's not a real race any more. The Cambridge team is drugged.'

He sat down on the bed, took off his glasses and pressed his eyelids for so long that I worried he might accidentally push his eyeballs too far into his skull and lose them forever.

'OK,' he said finally. 'You're absolutely right: we need to go to the police. Too bad about the race.'

I nodded and stood up. 'I'm proud of you, Will! A real sportsman.'

He had tears in his eyes. 'At least I've still got my little frogs,' he said, looking amorously at a picture on the wall of a little blue frog.

I turned around to look at it. 'It's very cute,' I said to make him feel better about it. 'It's got really good taste in colours, too. I'd love to wear electric blue clothes like that, but my parents will never let me, because their favourite colour is maroon and I always tell them ...'

I stopped, because I'd noticed a weird shadow on the wall. As if

someone behind me was raising their arms, holding something heavy …

And then I had a bit of a headache, and for the second time in less than a week, everything went █████████████████████████████
█████████████████████████████

X

'**H**ow dare he hit a skull that contains a brain that has as many connections in it as there are stars in the universe?'

This question remained unanswered, for I happened to be talking to a bunch of bags and luggage, which I could barely see anyway, as me and my dumb leathery companions were locked inside the boot of a van.

I don't know if you've ever been locked inside the boot of a van, but it's quite hustly and bustly in there. Not exactly the kind of place you'd elect for a cup of tea, unless you wanted

it to go everywhere but your mouth. And it's pretty cold, too. And it's pretty dark. And it's ferociously noisy.

And I'd been unconscious for long enough that I couldn't fall asleep again even if I tried. Technically, it's true that I was in a sleeping-bag, but the bag was zipped up and I was inside all tied up with rope, with just my eyes peering at the top, so the situation wasn't particularly doze-inducing.

'Ouch!' I ouched as the van braked and a bag flew at me and fell on top of my head.

This time, it felt like the van had stopped for good, as the engine died down. I wasn't sure how long I'd been unconscious, but I guessed we must have just arrived in London, where the crew was to stay in a hotel for the night. I heard the doors slamming, and Gwendoline's curt voice, muffled by the noise of the dying engine, saying, 'You get the bags out of the van, Wally.'

'Okey-doke, Gwen!' said Will's cheerful voice.

He opened the boot, and light flowed in.

'I'm awake!' I said.

'Shut up or you won't be awake for long,' he replied.

'I didn't have very good dreams,' I said. 'There was this lingering ache next to my ear, I wonder why.'

'I said shut up.'

'What are you going to do with me? Please don't kill me. My grandparents would be sad, I'm their only granddaughter.'

'I. Said. Shut. Up.'

He got all the bags out and hauled some on his shoulders.

'It's not very comfortable in here,' I said. 'On a scale of "bed of nails" to "mattress of pure cottonwool", it's much closer to the former.'

'Poor darling,' he groaned.

'I'm hungry, too. I haven't found the minibar.'

He rolled his eyes, and closed the boot again.

It's funny how reassuring a bunch of bags and suitcases can be.

You only realise it once you're all alone without any bags and suitcases around.

It's funny how reassuring the noise of the engine and the hustle and bustle of being driven around can be.

You only realise it once you're in a dark, quiet, motionless nothingness of a place.

'Don't panic, Sesame Seade,' I commanded. 'Don't think about panicking. Think about how to get out of the locked boot of a van when you're tied up in a sleeping bag in a manner very much resembling that of a sausage roll.'

I began to crawl along like a worm, and then decided to upgrade to caterpillar, getting my legs close to my head and then far again. The boot was big. I caterpillared my way through one side of it. Nothing there. Then the other, near the door, where I met some sort of cuddly toy that had been abandoned there. Then the next side, and finally the last ...

And that's when I bumped into something hard, which fell to the side with a metallic clunk, filling the place with an atrocious smell.

'Oh mirth and eternal joy,' I sighed. 'It's like being trapped in a locked room with Halitosis.

What is this repulsive stuff?'

This repulsive stuff was now slowly imbibing the side of the sleeping bag, and filtering through it all the way to my skin.

'Christ on a pair of purple rollerskates,' I cursed. 'Engine oil! Who keeps engine oil inside one's boot? Well, everyone, I guess, but still. I don't need any ointment, thank you very much, despite my sausage roll state.'

And now I was disgustingly oily.

'Well, at least,' I noted with some satisfaction, 'the oil has loosened the rope inside a little bit. It's definitely more comfortable this way. Maybe I'll even be able to sleep … Wait a minute. It's LOOSENING the ROPE!'

So I began to pull. And push. And tweak. And turn. And squiggle and wiggle and wriggle. And in the manner of the caterpillar slowly sliding out of its cocoon to emerge as a beautiful butterfly, I freed one hand, then the other hand, unzipped the zipper, and was OUT!

(Except, of course, that butterflies don't have hands and cocoons don't have zippers;

just pointing this out in case I get
accused of spreading falsities.)

'And now, my faithful mobile
phone, you're going to call Mum
and Dad,' I said.

I extracted the faithful mobile
phone from my pocket, and clicked
'Call Mum'.

'Unfortunately,' said a voice at
the other end of the line, 'it looks
like you haven't got enough credit
to make this call. Why not top up by
calling ...'

'Bother and double bother and triple
bother with bother cream on top,' I
pestered. 'All Gemma's fault for babbling
on about Toby's mosaic on the phone to
me the other time. Well, I can still call the
police, since emergency numbers don't
cost anything.'

So I dialled 999, and a voice on the other end of the line said, 'Hello there. It looks like you're calling us from a Phone4Kids phone. Are you a child? Are you sure you really want to call the emergency services? It's a very serious offence to call them if you're not really in a situation of emergency, you know. Have you told an adult that you're making this call? If not, you really should try and find an adult who can make it instead of you. If you really want to proceed to the emergency services, key 1.'

'Yes, yes, I do, you useless terrible atrocious not-in-the-least-useful phone,' I grumbled.

And I tried to press 1. Except my hands were covered in oil, so the phone joyfully leapt out of my fist in the manner of an Olympic diver, and crashed on to the floor of the boot, exploding into a great number of pieces, most of which drowned into the oil.

'I cannot believe this!' I shouted. 'The only time I want you alive and well, you go and die on me! You morbidly catastrophic piece of technology! You epically abominable machine

144

sent to destroy the Earth! I hate you and I hate the day my parents first laid eyes on you!'

My imprecations didn't seem to motivate the dead device to be alive again. I sat down, still as greasy as a French fry, and sulked. How dare Will do that to me? He who was so nice, so sweet. Will-Wally, always smiling, always positive, always—

'Wally,' I said to the dark boot. 'Wally. Why does that ring a bell?'

May I? interrupted my well-connected neurons in the form of a polite brain butler. *I should like to suggest that you were vaguely reminded of the* Where's Wally? *books the last time you saw that red-and-white woolly hat.*

'Yes, that's it,' I said. 'It did look like Wally's hat in the books. I was going to say it, but Toby interrupted me. What about it?'

Could it be because Will looks like Wally that he owns a red-and-white hat, perhaps as a joke from his fellow team members? Just a thought, of course, added my brain butler hastily.

'What do you mean?' I asked it. 'What's

Will got to do with that? It's Gwen and Julius's stolen jewellery in that hat.'

Well, Madam, whispered the amiable neuronal butler, *perhaps I wouldn't be so hasty. It struck me that the pirate described the zief, in fact, not as blond like Julius, but as brown-haired, like Toby. And like ...*

'... like WILL!' I shouted. 'Will, who's short, small and brown-haired! Will, who was the only one on the staircase with us when Gemma's earrings got stolen! Will, the jewellery thief? But why?'

I seem to recall that you said once that those burglaries might have been performed in order to pay for the poison, but I may be too ambitious in my hypothesis.

'The poison,' I murmured. 'Will would be the *poisoner*, too? But how?'

My brain butler coughed a little bit, and said, *I shall leave you to mull over it. As for myself, I think I have a frog in my throat.*

Frog.

FROG.

Will studies frogs.

Will studies how frogs' skins produce poison, which in turn can intoxicate humans by touching their skins.

Will, who could, with a little bit of money, buy more of the frogs, recently ...

... and gather enough of the poison to distil it, and put into something small and easy to carry, such as ...

'*A tube of antibacterial gel*!' I shouted. 'That's it! All the while we were thinking about food, all the while – but the poison was in the gel that Will was giving people to disinfect their hands! He gave it to Gemma, Toby and me as he was driving us home – he must have felt threatened by our findings – and I bet he did the same to Jeremy and Marcel as he drove them to the police station! Of course, things could have become a bit problematic for him if the police had seen the jewellery and traced it back to him ...'

But why? *Why* would he want the Cambridge team to be poisoned like that, when he was

clearly so keen to win the race that he'd locked me inside the boot of a van so that it wouldn't get cancelled?

Just as I was pondering upon this incomprehensible act of evil, crunchy noises outside the van indicated that two people were approaching.

'I can't find it anywhere,' said Gwendoline, 'so it must have fallen off my bag and be somewhere in the boot.'

'Are you sure you brought it?' asked Julius.

'Of course,' she scoffed. 'It's the team's mascot! Our little Cambridge teddy bear. I wouldn't have left it in Cambridge for the world.'

'Well,' said Julius, 'hurry up, we haven't got very long.'

Presently the boot opened, and there was light. And two faces topped with blonde hair.

'Sesame!' chorused the two siblings.

I would have replied, as I'm usually quite polite, but I didn't exactly have the time. As fast as lightning, I leapt out of the boot – but clearly

not fast enough, as Gwen caught me …

… and I slipped out of her arms like a bar of soap, in a splatter of oil!

Unlike my phone, I didn't shatter into pieces as I fell to the ground, but swiftly did a few forward rolls. Julius was right behind me as I got up again – but WHIZZ! – he slipped and skidded on the trail of oil that I'd left on the ground and SLAM! – he fell heavily on his back.

I ran away through the car park. The weather was all lovely and bright. The sun was nice and fresh in the sky like a tangerine sorbet. For a late afternoon sun, it didn't look tired at all.

In fact, it didn't look like a late afternoon sun. It looked just as if it was …

'The *morning*?' I gasped, running into one London street and then another, and tumbling down a flight of steps. 'It's Saturday morning? Then when Will opened the boot earlier, I'd slept the whole night in that van? But then it means …'

… and right then I had to stop as I'd reached a howling, screaming, laughing, cheering crowd,

149

glued to the barriers overlooking the River Thames ...

'... then it means ...'

... and I ran down bank after bank after bank of people pressed against each other, a tidal wave of dark blue and light blue, shaking flags in the air ...

'... then it means ...'

The Boat Race is NOW!

XI

'Sorry, Sir, but when does the Boat Race start?' I asked a random Oxford supporter, painted dark blue from head to toe in the manner of a Smurf.

'The men's first crews? They're racing in about ten minutes,' he said. 'The women's teams have just raced, Cambridge won. Look, the men are getting ready!' he added, pointing at a giant screen above the crowd.

Indeed on the screen everyone could see the Cambridge and the Oxford teams, all of them looking remarkably nervous, standing in two neat lines next to the river, surrounded by journalists. The poisonous Will Sutcliffe was there, equipped with his cox box, and just then Gwendoline

arrived and started to pat the shoulders of all the rowers in the Cambridge crew.

'And the coach of the Cambridge team is here,' roared the presenter, his voice magnified by the amplifiers on either side of the screen. 'Gwendoline Hawthorne, twenty-two years old, is encouraging her boys to beat Oxford! She also seems to be hugging what looks like an oily teddy bear. Anyway, in the midst of rumours about the general state of health of her team, it looks like Oxford may have got the psychological advantage ...'

'Where is it?' I asked hurriedly. 'The starting-point of the race?'

'Oh, up there,' said the Oxford fan, pointing vaguely at the river. 'But I wouldn't go there,

if I were you – no point! You won't see anything. You should stay here and watch them pass by!'

'I'm not interested in watching them pass by. I'm interested in stopping them from racing!' I exclaimed, and started to run.

Well, that was the intention. Because I ran into a very compact group of Cambridge supporters, crawled between their legs, emerged within a wave of Oxford fans, squeezed between them, and proceeded in this extremely inconvenient fashion until I finally managed to pop out of the giant crowd and actually start to run.

Seven minutes now! And I had no idea how far I was from the starting-point. If only I'd had my rollerskates! But that treacherous Will must have left them in his room.

So I had to run.

In my socks.

The problem is, whether in socks or not, as you may or may not know – and I admit it freely,

because I have many other qualities – I'm not a very good runner.

Not a very good runner … at … all.

Not … even … a little … bit.

I'd managed a minute and a half of sprinting before it started feeling like I was about to spit out my own lungs, while both my kidneys were shattering into millions of pieces, not to mention my extraordinarily painful knee joints. In my mind I could hear Mr Halitosis shouting at me, 'Faster, Sophie Seade, faster! Your jogging style reminds me of a seal hauling itself on to an iceberg!'

I understood now that he was cruelly right.

Panting, I stopped somewhere along the bank and wheezed and coughed and cursed myself. Ah! Wouldst that I were a professional marathon runner! But alas, not a drop of that talent in my otherwise excellent blood: it had to let other people have their chance too.

Leaning over the barrier, I spotted the starting-point of the Boat Race. It was astronomically far from where I was standing.

155

No way at all I'd get there in five minutes.

It was all over. The criminal Cambridge team would race with a criminal cox and a criminal coach.

I couldn't stop them.

Unless ...

Unless I could somehow get to that little Zodiac that was moored down there near the river.

Unless I could get to it before its owner, who was standing on the bank looking at the river through binoculars, noticed what I was doing.

Unless I could get to it and manage to find out how to make it start before anyone could stop me.

I had to be fast.

'Hey! Hey, you! That kid's just jumped on my boat! Hey!'

'Come on,' I whispered to the engine, 'come on, how do you work? How do you start?'

And once again my fabulously well-connected brain saved the day, because it somehow seemed to remember what it had seen

156

Gwendoline do the other day on the motorboat in Ely, even though I couldn't even remember looking at her then.

It told me calmly to turn the key into the ignition.

It then told me to pull on the rope, several times, until the engine started to putt-putt in the manner of Dad having found Peter Mortimer's offering of half a squirrel on his pillow.

It then told me to grab on to the rudder.

And then it told me to GO!

SPLASH! went the water behind me as the owner of the Zodiac fell into the Thames while trying to jump on to his boat.

VROOM! went the Zodiac on the water in a very straight line until I figured out how to steer it.

It was going slightly faster than a falling meteorite, and stood almost vertical on the water, but supersleuths like me are endowed with a splendid sense of balance. In about twelve seconds, I was as wet as a halibut.

Of course, I couldn't

resist doing a few circles on the water and then accelerating a little bit more, but you wouldn't have resisted it either.

But I did remember that I was on a mission.

Conveniently, the starting-point of the race was getting closer and closer – and to my horror, I spotted the two teams settling into the boats and strapping their feet into place.

So I slashed through the water, slaloming around the journalists' boats, speeding up nearer and nearer to the start …

'Stop that boat!' shouted someone.

'And there seems to be an incident near the start of the Boat Race,' said the voice of the presenter in the amplifiers. 'An unidentified Zodiac is absolutely rushing towards the Cambridge and Oxford boats … Oh my goodness! It's going to hit them! … No, it isn't! It's braking! … It's stopping near the bank … Well, the police are now running down in full gear to welcome our unwanted guest …'

Silence.

Then:

'What on Earth … ? It's a *little girl*!'

There wouldn't have been more police officers if I'd been trying to steal the Queen. I looked up, half-expecting to see a dozen more parachuting down with loaded Kalashnikovs, but unfortunately I only saw seagulls and pigeons.

In the middle of the river, the two long rowing-boats were rocked by the downwash from my Zodiac, but all the rowers and the two coxes were staring at the bank. On the bank, there was me, there were journalists, there were the police, and a crowd of hundreds of people, each of them staring at me with eyes like this: O O.

You know me. I'm not completely against being the centre of attention.

'Hello hello!' I chanted. 'Sorry to interrupt. May I borrow a microphone?'

'She's asking for a microphone!' exclaimed the presenter's voice through the speakers. 'Who *is* this kid?'

Two police officers were already

frogmarching me to the top of the bank, but a murmur rose from the crowd of journalists. One BBC presenter with a camera drew closer to us, shouting, 'She's a little girl! You can't arrest her like that, in front of the whole country!'

'I'm not in the least little,' I pointed out; 'in fact I'm quite tall for my age, which is eleven and a half years old.'

I was now surrounded with cameras and journalists, and could see my own face on the huge screen above. Shame about the oil and the water, which made my hair all sleek and tidy instead of letting it express its usual wild personality.

Meanwhile, the journalists were

throwing interesting questions at me:

'What are you trying to do by this action? Where are your parents? Have you stolen this boat? Are you protesting against the perpetuation of sheer elitism and class supremacy which the Oxford–Cambridge Boat Race embodies as an annual reminder and celebration of the hegemony of the intellectual ruling classes?'

I said, 'Let me explain.'

And then there was silence, and I saw that it was good.

So I went on:

'Friends, Londonians, countrymen. And countrywomen. And countrychildren. This Boat Race is rigged! The Cambridge crew is integrally doped. Without the rowers' knowledge, their coach, Gwendoline Hawthorne, helped by her brother Julius, has been mixing performance-enhancing drugs into their food. On top of that, their cox, Will Sutcliffe, also known as Wally, has, for reasons unclear, been steadily poisoning some selected members of the first

crew, and also some unsuspecting members of the public, such as me, my sidekicks, my Editor-in-Chief, and a pirate. In order to pay for the poison, which he administered through the skin by the means of fake antibacterial gel, he robbed jewellery from barges on the Cam for over a month.'

No noise was to be heard, apart from the clicking of the cameras and the seagulls' laughter. It was super satisfying.

'To sum up,' I concluded, 'this Boat Race cannot be allowed to take place!'

And suddenly the noise was deafening, and I was carried away by the policemen who had greeted me, while the presenter's voice above my head was screaming, 'And it looks like the race is delayed! The two crews have been asked to row back to the bank and disembark! Are they about to drug-test them? Drug-testing rowers in the Boat Race is incredibly rare – could this child be right?'

It was much quieter inside the room where the officers took me, and where I had to reveal

to them a variety of tedious details such as my name, date of birth, and where on Earth my parents may be.

'They must be at home in Cambridge,' I said. 'But probably not watching the Boat Race, so I wouldn't worry; like every Saturday morning, Dad must be writing a sermon and Mum must be doing some equations to relax. I'll be back before they even notice I've been up to something.'

But the police officer insisted on calling them. It wasn't wise, as he almost lost his eardrum once he'd told Dad about what I'd been up to. From the other side of the room, even I heard what Dad said, and it wasn't a bunch of words he would have happily repeated in front of his church-goers.

'Your parents are coming to fetch you,' he said after hanging up, massaging his ear.

'Well, that's good, I guess. I didn't feel like another ride in that sleeping-bag.'

'They're not very pleased,' he pointed out.

'They very rarely are. Even when I got first

prize at kindergarten for best robot made out of toilet rolls, they were just like, "Have you learnt to read yet?". Of course I had already, but I didn't tell them because I'm not the kind to brag about being able to read at three years old, even though one must admit it's quite exceptional.'

'I see. You're a bit of a handful, aren't you?' he murmured.

'Police officers in Cambridge have just called,' said a policewoman walking into the room. 'They've found child-sized rollerskates in Will Sutcliffe's room, as well as the stolen jewellery and tubes of antibacterial gel, which is currently being analysed. They've been to the cellars of St Catharine's and have found a chest with bags of powder in it, which is also being analysed.'

'Well,' said the policeman, 'looks like your version of the events is slowly being corroborated, young lady.'

'Of course, since nothing in the whole history of the world has ever been truer than

what I said. Have you got any food, preferably chocolate-based? If not, I'll have to resort to eating my own arm.'

Happily, they had a whole box of teacakes, which I tucked into ravenously, covering the floor with little balls of foil wrapping and my face with chocolate. My arm, meanwhile, was sighing with relief that it wasn't going to get munched on.

'The journalists want to see the girl again,' said the policewoman a little bit later, looking completely exhausted.

'Duty calls!' I sighed, following her outside. 'It's the ransom of success.'

I answered a million questions. I told them about being a sausage roll in the boot of a van, about frog-racing, about being kidnapped

by pirates, and about the terrible loss of my Phone4Kids phone. I told them about Gemma's earrings which she should really get back or else she'd lose her power over adults, and about poor Jeremy who must be watching this between two fits of sickness; hello Jeremy! In short, I told them everything.

Finally the police got the phone call from Cambridge confirming that the antibacterial gel indeed contained poison, and that the powder in the chest was indeed dope. The drug tests on the Cambridge crew revealed that they were all drugged. So Will and Gwendoline were swiftly driven to the guillotine and beheaded.

Well, not really, but they did end up in court, just like their fellow law-breakers arrested in my previous adventures.

And then there was an Announcement:

'Ladies and gentlemen. Due to recent developments, the Cambridge team has no cox, no coach and no crew. As a result, they are forfeiting. The Boat Race cannot take place, and Oxford is this year's winner by default.'

'NOT SO FAST!' howled a voice in the crowd.

Everyone turned around, and my jaw dropped so low that I felt the soft caress of the wet floor on my chin.

'*Mr Halitosis?*'

XII

'There seems to be a new development,' said the presenter in the microphone, 'as what looks like a group of eight primary school children, accompanied by their ... erm ... relatively big-boned teacher, are now making their way to the bank!'

'This race must be run!' spluttered Mr Halitosis into a journalist's microphone. 'I mean, rowed. Well, you know what I mean. It must be rowed by people who know the meaning of hard work and effort! It must be rowed by people who aren't drugged!'

'Well,' I said, 'if you mean us, we have been eating Mr Appleyard's food for five years.'

'Hush, Sophie!' he said. 'Ladies and

gentlemen, I bring you the Cambridge team that will row against Oxford!'

And he gestured towards our crew, calling, 'Gemma! Lily! Solal! Emerald! Ben! Jamie! Kristina! and at Bow, Toby! and as Cox, Sophie!'

'And after all, why not?' said the presenter's voice as everyone around us was mumbling and muttering in the manner of light and dark blue bees. 'We all came to see a race!'

'We saw you on TV,' whispered Toby to me, 'and we thought it was a shame to waste a good opportunity to row. So we called everyone and Mr Halitosis.'

'But you hate rowing!'

'I know,' he said. 'I'll have to get over it, though. At least for today.'

He would indeed, as the two rowing boats, the dark Oxford blue and the light Cambridge blue, were being wheeled out of the hangar again!

And Will's cox box was being strapped around my head!

And a few minutes later, I was facing

Gemma, at stroke, and the whole of the River Thames, and the whole of the UK, in our boat, rocked by the waves, parallel to the Oxford boat, and eagerly waiting for the starting shot to go—

...

...

...

POW!

'Don't say we won, Sesame. It would be a lie. And it's easy for anyone to check, anyway.'

'OK, all right, we didn't win. But we finished!'

'We did. And not very long after the Oxford crew!'

'Not very long at all! Well, they had time to have a little shower.'

'A biggish shower, yes. And a sandwich.'

'Maybe a sandwich or two. But we finished!'

'We did! You can say that in the book.'

Following Gemma's advice, I'm not going to pretend we won. But then you wouldn't have

believed me, would you? I only have clever readers.

But there was so much lashing and washing and slashing of the waves!

So many screams and shouts and howls and lung-splitting calls from the banks!

So many cold slaps of wind and freezing splashes and splatters of water!

'Come on, team!' I roared. 'Up one, down one! Let's get it up to thirty-eight! And … PUSH FOR TEN!'

(No one knew what it meant, myself included, but it seemed to work.)

Never had my crew rowed so fast and for so long!

Never had they been so focused on victory!

Never had they been so brave and so breathless!

And even the greasy, sweaty, faint-inducingly smelly hug of Halitosis was worth it for passing the finish line.

And even Mum and Dad's deadly glares of laser and fire, which accidentally killed fifteen

172

passers-by and seriously injured three others, were worth it for being carried by the crowd in a shower of champagne.

'If I see you opening your mouth and swallowing as little as an atom of alcohol, Sophie Seade,' I heard Mum shout from below, 'you will be … you will be … well, you'll be sorry!'

So I kept my mouth completely shut, but then I licked the corners of my lips when she wasn't looking.

And then we were given consolatory medals, congratulated by the Oxford crew, covered with safety blankets, asked another million questions, and finally, before I could say 'Well done team!' I was scooped up by Dad and carried away to the Smurfmobile, in which I fell instantly asleep.

'Knock knock!'

'Come in, it's open.'

I pushed the door a little bit and was happy

to note that Jeremy's sickness hadn't changed him a bit: his bedroom still looked like it had been traversed by two or three typhoons.

'Hello, my favourite Editor-in-Chief of all time!' I called melodiously, and sat down on a chair next to his bed. 'How long since you last threw up?'

'Five hours and fifty-two minutes,' he said weakly.

'Ah, you're almost cured. I'm glad you've kept yourself occupied by doing some maggot-rearing. Oh, sorry, no, it's just a discarded sandwich that got colonised.'

'I still can't believe you threw me into the arms of a poisoner,' he groaned.

'I didn't know at the time! I thought he was perfectly adorable. How's the essay going? The one that's due last week?'

'I can't find the sheet on which the essay question's written,' he said.

'Could it be that one on the desk that you used as a plate for very old fried onion rings?'

'It could be,' he admitted. 'I wouldn't check

if I were you. Anyway, how's celebrity treating you?'

'Rubbishly. Fame is a fickle friend, Jeremy – remember that. Not one article on me today! The whole thing died down after four days.'

'Cruel fate. You'll have to go back to being Chief Investigator for *UniGossip*.'

'I never left,' I asserted. 'Meanwhile, you said you had my skates and Gemma's earrings?'

'Yes, they're over there somewhere,' he said. 'I got a friend at Homerton to pick them up for you.'

I found one rollerskate hidden under a pile of laundry and the other one in an empty box of chicken nuggets. I kissed and hugged them and promised them I'd never leave them alone again. The earrings were trickier to find, but after fifteen minutes of turning everything over, Jeremy remembered he'd put them inside one of the rollerskates so he wouldn't forget where he'd put them.

'Well, Sesame,' said Jeremy, sitting up, 'you've done it again. Supersleuthed your way

to the front page of next week's *UniGossip*.'

He showed me the dummy front page, and it was a picture of me in the cox's seat, all oily and wet, with the headline 'Boat Race Scandal: Smartypant Supersleuth Stops Cheats, Steals Sutcliffe's Seat and Steers Ship!'

'Ah, I'm megaproud. Next to that, being on BBC Breakfast or in the *New York Times* is rubbish.'

'But that's not all there is to this special issue,' he said. 'I phoned the place where Will Sutcliffe is detained, and managed to obtain an exclusive interview with him.'

'Wicked! Were you sick in the middle of it?'

'Twice,' he admitted, 'but I still got him to answer my most pressing question: why did he poison people from the crew?'

'And?'

'And he told me everything.'

Long pause.

'Come on, Jeremy, stop being a dramatic little Sarah something.'

'OK. Well, here's the truth. He felt constantly humiliated. Since someone first started calling him Wally, all the boys in the first crew kept laughing at him and mocking him. They were so much bigger than him, too, you know – he couldn't do anything. One evening, six of them dressed him up as Wally – that's where he got the hat from – and carried him around Cambridge, from pub to pub. They played a little 'game', hiding him in places and asking people to look for him, shouting, "Where's Wally?" and ridiculing him. Will had had enough. He decided to avenge himself by kicking those six boys out of the first crew. He distilled some frog poison – just enough that it would make them

sick for a week or so. He knew that by that time, they'd already lost the chance to catch up with training. But then it went a bit too far, he thought he was going to be found out, and started poisoning more people.'

He looked at me, and we stayed silent for a while, listening to the joyful slurpy noises that the maggots were making at the foot of Jeremy's bed.

'So there you go,' he concluded. 'His pride was wounded. That's the way he found of restoring his dignity.'

'Bit silly of him, really,' I said. 'Would you mind it a lot if people compared you to a character from a children's book?'

'Of course I would!' scoffed Jeremy.

'Well, I wouldn't,' I said. 'Nothing could please me more. Anyway, Editor, Sir, I need to go home and catch up on all the homework, and then go see Gemma to give her earrings back to her and repair her broken heart.'

I stood up and immediately yawned.

'Tired?' asked Jeremy.

'No. Bored. It's been four days without a mission. Got any more in stock?'

'Not right now, no – I've been in bed with frog poisoning, in case you hadn't noticed.'

I shrugged, and left his bedroom with a weight on my chest that comes from the formidable boredom of profound idleness. Those Editors-in-Chief who name you Chief Investigator and then don't give you anything to Investigate, just because they've got a little stomach problem! What is a restless supersleuth to do?

I left Gonville & Caius College and was putting on my faithful rollerskates to go back to Christ's, when a hand fell on to my shoulder, and a low voice behind me said into my ear:

'Miss Sesame Seade?'

'I do answer to that name,' I replied. 'Who are you?'

'Important people who think you could be very useful to us.'

'How so?' I asked. 'Would you like to learn to skate?'

'Not quite. We would like you to help us investigate the claim that Mr Jeremy Hopkins, of Gonville & Caius College, Cambridge, may be ...'

'May be what? A bit lazy? A bit unable of tidying up his room?'

'No. An internationally-wanted criminal.'

I whistled.

And then I thought about it for a minute.

Until I eventually said, 'OK, then, sounds like my kind of mission.'

And I raised a menacing finger:

'But I do need to catch up on my homework first.'

Acknowledgements

This Sesame book could not have been written without experience of a year-and-a-half of very mediocre, but very motivated rowing. I fondly remember the shouts of our cox Jo Hardley, the boxes of chocolate before and after races, and the smelly changing-rooms. I was lucky enough to attend an outing in Ely of the Men's Lightweights, which informed the equivalent episode in this book - thank you, Sarah Smart and your team, for having me!

I am also extremely grateful to Danny Longman for sharing his inside knowledge about the Boat Race – and particularly his revelation that there are, indeed, no drug tests in this competition.

Questions with the French, Freckled and Fringed Author

1. How is your name pronounced?
Clementeen Bovay. But you can call me Clem.

2. What inspired you to write about Sesame?
Walking around Cambridge, I thought it would be really fun to be a child there and explore all the secret passages and sneak into forbidden rooms. I'd also always wanted to write a mystery story, and to create a superheroine without superpowers – so I put it all together and Sesame was born.

3. Were you at all like her as a child?
Yes and no. For a start, I couldn't skate at all! I was always on my scooter, though, like Gemma. Like Sesame, I always hated PE at school, couldn't run to save my life, and kept passing little notes to my best friends during class. My teachers were much better-smelling than Mr Halitosis though! I loved animals, like

Sesame, and also had a cat. But otherwise my life couldn't have been more different – I lived in Paris, my parents were much more relaxed and cool than Sesame's, and I certainly wasn't crazy enough to escape at night and do anything like roof-climbing. I was also very bookish and well-behaved! I think I was much more boring than Sesame.

4. Do you have as many middle names as she does?

I even have one more - my full name is Clémentine Morgane Mélusine Hécate Beauvais. In France it's quite normal to have three middle names, but mine are completely fanciful – they're names of famous enchantresses and witches of folklore and mythology. My dad's idea...

5. What is the most embarrassing thing your parents ever did to you when you were twelve?

My dad sings extremely loudly in the streets and in the underground, where, according to him, 'the acoustic is better'. I can't count the number of times I bumped into friends while my father was singing opera tunes at the top of his falsetto voice, going up escalators in the Paris metro or just walking down the street. I was mortified every time. Sesame's father would never dream of doing that!

6. If any readers were to visit Cambridge, where should they go?

Visiting the colleges is a nice thing to do – look up and try to spot the gargoyles, the holes and crevices in the walls, the swirly staircases behind half-open doors … Cambridge is also full of lovely small museums: go to the Sedgwick Museum of Earth Sciences – it's packed with dinosaur bones and odd fossils. Then rent a punt, canoe or kayak and go to Grantchester if the weather's nice – it's a brilliant place to have a picnic.

Sesame picks up her skates...

GARGOYLES gone A.W.O.L

A Sesame Seade Mystery

CLÉMENTINE BEAUVAIS

Illustrated by SARAH HORNE

Sesame takes to the rooftops!